BO

HEXINGTON FALLS:

THE HEART OF MARE

MIGUEL T. PINTOS

For my wife and two boys

"We are all fighting through something in our lives. No matter how big or small. Create something that may help others push through."

-Miguel T. Pintos

INTRO

"In the 1400's, humans hunted down the supernatural. Village by village, every monster was slaughtered whether they were wicked or not. Their state of extinction brought on a war. The more civilized beings of the supernatural agreed to protect these creatures that were created by the heart of mare. They formed a group of the more powerful witches and wizards to combine their magic and sacrifice themselves to open a rift to a new world which they called Purgintor. Due to having more of a human appearance, many of the magical beings stood within the human realm.

During the 1600's in Salem and many other places around the world, these magical beings were being hunted and killed. They had no choice but to retreat to Purgintor. Some monsters who did not like the idea of hiding from the humans, took advantage of the magical tech that was invented by the brilliant minds of their world. They created portals, to sneak back to the human realm and terrorize all its people. The leaders of Hexington Falls and surrounding towns assigned rangers to keep up the law in their world and keep the radicals from passing through the realms. Many creatures tried but failed. Overtime, some ended up succeeding, finding their way through the human world which influenced the idea of forming teams that were filled with the best hunter's, men and women, to search and extract all of the individuals who passed through illegally. One of the teams was known as the Nocturnal Squad.

Chapter 1

A long time ago…

Día de los Muertos… It was the day of the dead.

"I finally got you, you son of a--," the pale hunter stated, but before he could finish his full statement, the sly creature that the man was chasing made a run for it, again.

Almost everyone in town was at the festival, therefore all the houses and streets in the small neighborhoods were deserted. The fanged hunter chased the monster down several empty streets as the beast made a dash toward a nearby home. It had picked up a human scent. "Damn, everyone was supposed to be at the festival!"

The vampire picked up his speed. He was not going to lose another human, not to this beast. He'd been chasing this creature all over the Caribbean and Latin America. He was so close this time and refused to let it escape him again. The beast disappeared into the tiny house and the hunter followed behind. Once inside, he saw it. Many know it as the boogeyman but in Mexico, they called it El Cucuy. It loomed over a sleeping girl, innocent and unaware of the beast that was just above. The foul beast licked his lips and began to open its mouth.

"Not this time," the man growled while he lifted his weapon, needing not even a second to aim as he shot.

The beast hit the floor, shot straight through the head. The sudden noise startled the little girl awake and she sat up suddenly. The vampire stepped up to her calmly, revealing a badge that was strapped to his waist. She looked into the vampire's eye and at his thick mustache as she tried to see if she knew him from somewhere.

"It's okay, go back to sleep. Everything is going to be alright," he told her, trying to convince her that she was safe. The little girl tilted her head to the side and somehow decided that he was to be trusted and fell back asleep. Little did he know, she was very ill and could hardly stay awake let alone carry on a conversation.

Suddenly a voice from behind exclaimed, "What the hell is going on here?!"

ONE YEAR AGO...

There was no time to think, only to run. Nearly gasping for air as he scurried through the foggy woods, the old caretaker for the local Sleepy Hollow Cemetery, raced for his life. He focused on reaching the nearby church close to the burial ground. He pushed on as fast as his tired old legs would carry him under the low hanging trees. Sharp pain pierced his side and coursed through his legs. The countless trees seemed never-ending as their branches grew every way. With only the half-moon as his guiding light that night, he was left to hope that he could make it back to safety before it was too late. As he made his way down the winding dirt path between the trees, he continuously tried to avoid the grabbing branches and roots that had been sticking up from the ground. He had been stumbling with every cut, scrape, and smack. However, in the distance, hooves pounded hard against the ground. He could hear the crunching of the roots and the sound of the branches being torn away. The speeding creature was getting closer as it carried its rider toward their next target.

"Help!" the man cried out knowing there would be no response at that time of night. The pounding of the hooves grew louder as the ground began to shake. "Somebody, HELP!" the caretaker begged out into the void. There was no aid in sight and no hope of anyone close enough to have heard his cries. His hope for survival diminished more and more with every frightening sound.

An eerie echo laugh whipped with the wind, reaching the old man. He looked back, terrified, and unaware of a root that grew as an arch, reaching out from the ground and diving back into the earth. The Caretaker tripped and hit the hard forest path floor. His body rolled in the dirt, nearly out of energy, he managed to pull himself off the ground. This time he did not dare to look back. He did not care about his scraped shin or the blood that trickled down his face. He took a step, ready to run again, but his knee was quick to give out. Frozen with fear, he was hesitant to move.

The forest was quiet. Even the bugs and the birds seemed to fear whatever was lurking in the night. A large gust of wind blew through the trees and ripped off leaves, forcing them to the ground. The scared man squinted his eyes, focusing only on the direction he knew could bring him to safety.

He felt something crawling on his arm and jumped suddenly. The paranoia was setting in and he knew it as he looked down to see only a spider. He flicked the arachnid off him. He continued to listen while looking into the darkness. He could feel the silence that surrounded him. It felt like a forest that was empty with only a hunter and prey.

The man tried to think of how he got this deep into the woods. There was no memory of how he got there. His last thoughts were of him going on break and slowly falling asleep in the back of his truck as his portable T.V played an old horror movie. The caretaker tried convincing himself that this was all a bad dream, but the pain that his old body was feeling told him otherwise. There was only one logical thought he had left, *"Did I sleepwalk?"*

CRACK! a branch behind him snapped. His eyes widened while the hairs on the back of his neck stood as a chill shot up his spine. He slowly looked back to see whatever may have been behind him. As the man turned, he saw nothing but darkness. Nobody was there. Only the inky forest threatening him through the soldiers of trees. The moon was not bright enough to pierce through shields of leaves and thick branches. He squinted in the direction he knew the noise was coming from.

The old man turned quietly as he tried to continue his way toward the sanctuary when suddenly, out swiped a sword just above his head. It had nearly cut him down where he stood!

SWOOP! He dodged the blade again, but not without having stumbled backwards and hitting the ground. The man's throat was dry, and he could not find his voice to scream. His eyes were blinded by a flaming sword. They quickly adjusted to the fire as he saw the dark figure of a headless being that towered over him. The body wore a large torn black trench coat that had blended into the darkness of the night. He noticed the sword's cross guard hilt had a Jack-O-Lantern carved on the bottom and the rest of the hilt looked as if the pumpkin had roots that swirled around the top of it. The blade under the flames seemed massive. All together the weapon looked heavy so he could only imagine how strong this being really was. Behind the rider was a massive shadow-like creature. As it was noticed, the red-eyed beast had let out a thunderous neigh. The enormous undead horse-like creature lifted its front legs into the air, standing on its hind legs. The beast was magnificent as it too seemed to vanish into the surrounding darkness. It was only visible from the fire blade and sinister red eyes that looked as if they were floating in midair. The horseman's burning blade reached toward the underbelly of the leaf barrier above as lightning flickered through the cracks within the leaves overhead.

The rider swung his blade to strike the old man, but once more, the caretaker quickly rolled over and avoided his demise. Adrenaline rushed through him and forced the injured man back up and he pushed onward, running. The horseman climbed back onto his monstrous steed and rode toward his prey.

11

The caretaker barely managed to make his way out of the dense trees and ran toward a rickety old wooden bridge that spanned over a brook. Behind him was the notorious legend of Sleepy Hollow, racing toward him, after exploding out of the fog.

All the blood-curdling stories he'd been told as a child were in fact, real. The myth that people told children before bed was going to be the thing that took his life. His legs had cramps and his lungs were burning as he continued gasping for air. The caretaker had no choice other than to fight through the pain and lack of oxygen if he wanted any chance at staying alive through the night.

The horseman rode closer and closer, each second as his steed's heels pounded the soil beneath its weight. The smell of smoke grew stronger as the old man realized that he was seconds away from his death. He closed his eyes in defeat, as he started to slow down, while breathing what he thought would be his final breath. He had accepted his fate.

Just behind him, the horseman raised his sword into the night as he readied himself for the final blow, when- *BAM!* A quick blur tackled the hunter off his midnight steed. The caretaker heard the commotion behind him. As he turned around, he saw the horse with no rider. The devilish steed continued moving rapidly toward the caretaker with its beaming red eyes that had locked onto nothing but the old man.

The powerful driven horse was just seconds away from crushing the man. The caretaker braced himself for what was about to happen, but then he felt his body lift into the air as he suddenly flew sideways, moving out of harm's way. The steed missed its target and leapt up onto its hind legs letting out a cry of failure. The caretaker found himself somehow alive, gliding towards the ground. He could feel the cold touch from a hand that was still holding onto him.

The old man looked up to investigate who his savior was. There was a woman looking down at him. She was beautiful with dark straight hair whipping behind them as they continued soaring. Her eyes were a reddish brown, surrounded by olive pale skin. To his surprise, she looked young. Must be in her mid-twenties like his granddaughter. She wore a dark skintight suit that allowed her to move with ease. The mystery woman appeared ready for combat. The caretaker eyed her holster attached to her back. It held what seemed like a small metal staff. There was no doubt that the woman was quite extraordinary, to move the man out of the way that fast and effortlessly. How did this stranger have the strength to move him with such force and without breaking a sweat? She made it seem as easy as picking up a doll.

The two finally come to a safe spot where the woman could let him go. "Get out of here now!" Lyra, his savior, ordered him. The caretaker nods his head and flees the scene as quickly as he can. He didn't need to be told twice.

He looked back, only to see the villainous horseman as he got up from the ground while another figure stood just across from him. This one was similar to the woman, with a black tactical look, but a broader muscular frame. His posture was beastly, wolf-like without all the hairiness and face distortion. He had some type of tech that he wrapped around his wrist. A small blue light was consistently blinking from the device. His eyes glowed yellow as they stayed fixated on the horseman he was circling, ready to attack. "Cedric, be careful!" Lyra cried out as she rushed over to assist him.

The horseman reached for his sword and started to move towards the wolfman. Cedric growled at the sinister rider, then darted in for his attack. The horseman swung his sword, but the wolf slid under and through the rider's legs. From behind, Cedric swung his leg against the horseman's which made him unbalanced.

The steed ran in headfirst and knocked the wolfman to the ground as he went skidding against the dirt, knocking him away from its master.

When Cedric was not looking, the rider swung his fire blazing sword in his direction, but Lyra jumped forward and pulled a baton looking piece from her holster. The piece cut through the air as it had suddenly shot open to full size. She manipulated the heavy magically welded staff, that was taller than her own body, to hold against the horseman's blade. Caught off guard, Cedric looked back and saw Lyra had a smirk across her face, showing off two perfect white fangs.

"Good lookin' out, Fangs," Cedric grinned playfully as he jumped back up on his feet and was ready to attack.

"Don't thank me just yet," she shot back, eyes focused on the rider, but the grin was still there. "We still have to get our little *friend* here back to his cell."

Lyra pushed forward with all her weight. The horseman was forced backward as the vampire started to strike over and over. With every jab of her staff, the rider was on the defense. He was quick to block each strike with the burning sword, but never faster than she was to get off a full hit. Although Lyra was fast, the heat of her attacker's sword was beginning to get closer until finally she jumped back to avoid a block that was too close to her face.

The headless horseman saw the opening and did not waste a second to go in for the stab. Lyra leapt over him to avoid the flaming blade and landed behind him with a spin and powerful kick to his back. The horseman stumbled, but regained his balance as the rider swung his sword all the way around to strike her. Lyra leapt up into the air, avoiding the blade while Cedric jumped in to tackle the horseman to the ground. The vampire approached the rider and pulled the sword from him. She glanced at it for a second but tossed it to the ground and instead took out her own staff and pierced it into the center of his chest. She dug the staff into his chest, letting him know that he was beaten.

"It's over bro," Cedric stated proudly to the headless rider. The monster tried to get up, but he could barely move, when suddenly, there was an orange glow slithering around its headless body.

"Like my friend just said, it's over," a voice of a Wizard echoed, from the darkness. A white, small light emerged from the shadows. Soon, a figure could be seen with a casting light leading whomever it was toward the group. The figure moved closer and soon they could make out a black tactical suit like Cedric's, only there was an olive leather jacket over top of this one. Finally, he stepped out into the opening to expose his clean-shaven face and gentleman's haircut. He held his white illuminated energy wand in the air at the horseman while he had cast a spell to try and contain the headless creature.

"Took you long enough Mitch," Lyra said while she rolled her eyes.

"Sorry, I was just enjoying the show. Looked as if you guys had everything under control," Mitchell snickered back with a smirk on his face.

"Alright, let's get *Mr. Headless* back to where he belongs. Mitch, open the portal," Cedric said as he was focused on finishing their mission.

Mitchell did not disagree and tossed a flat metal device just a few feet from the group. The wizard could not help but gaze down at his arm. A mysterious glow bloomed from his forearm tattoo. Confident, he turned his attention back on the creature and his wand that was already pointed at the bonded horseman. Mitch reached his other arm out towards the device and turned his focus toward it. His eyes narrowed, concentrating, when suddenly a green spark popped off the metal object. The wizard focused harder, letting go of everything around him. Then more green sparks shot out and danced above the device, becoming larger and larger as they swirled into circles, slowly connecting until they created the portal to Purgintor.

SNAP! Mitch heard an unwelcoming noise. He, along with the team, prepared for whatever they would need to fight, only to see the caretaker spying on them from a slight distance. Mitch noticed the man's eyes reflected an emerald glow. Unaware, the rift slowly began to close as the wizard leaned in to get a better look at the human. The old man was just standing there, frozen like an animal ready for death. Mitch saw the man's face and fear etched into each wrinkle.

"Excuse me sir, but I'm going to have to ask you to move along for your own safety." Still fixated on the emerald glow, the Wizard had forgotten something else that was worthy of his attention.

While everyone's eyes were on the old man, the legendary villain was the very first to notice the spell keeping him bound, had worn off. He snagged his sword beneath him before anyone could have even bothered to think of him, let alone stopped him. The horseman had slowly approached Mitchell from behind. He moved with the wind, so quiet and stealthy, unnoticed by the wizard who had been too focused on the pathetic old man. Without any warning from the wind or trees, the headless monster forced his blade straight through Mitchell's body.

Lyra and Cedric turned just in time to see the wizard's body lock up, eyes toward the sky as he suddenly tried to gasp for a painful breath. The flaming blade ripped out of him, letting gravity take his body to the cold floor.

17

Both of his team-mates just watched. They could not find the thought process to move. Shock slammed in as Mitchell's body lay on the ground. Lyra was the first to break out of the trance and rush toward the horseman. With anger coursing through her, she whipped her staff through the air. The vampire could not help, but yelled out as she took the killer out viciously. The horseman tried to get back up but as he grabbed his sword. Lyra with all her strength, stomps on the blade, breaking the pointed tip half right off. Cedric ran to Mitchell's aid, unsure of what he would see of his friend. He ripped off the olive coat, exposing a deep laceration. The poison from the blade was acting fast in the wizard's weak body. Cedric winced as he applied pressure to the hole pooled with blood on his friend's chest.

Lyra finished restraining the horseman before she ran toward Cedric and Mitchell's side. Mitch looked up as Lyra rushed toward him and dropped to her knees. Exhausted, Cedric leaned back and wiped his face, painting it with the blood of the wizard.

While blood was dripping from his lips and he struggled to speak, Mitch grabbed Lyra's hand and whispered, "Give this to my brother." Mitchell struggled, but he reached his arm and wrapped his fingers in the collar of his jacket. He pulled, using any bit of strength he had left, and placed it in Lyra's hands. The wizard let his head drop to the cold ground and his body finally seemed to relax. Mitch's eyes fluttered shut as he tried to catch his breath.

"H-he always liked it… and it m-might look better… on him than m…me," The wizard spit out in between breaths. He forced a smile that exposed his blood-stained teeth. A tear slid out his eye and down toward his hair, taking all the sweat, dirt, and blood in its path with it.

Lyra could not help as a few tears slipped past her eyelashes as she felt Mitchell's strong hand become limp in her grasp. "No," she whimpered out, this time unable to stop the soft cries that followed.

"M-Mitch...hey!" Cedric placed his hand on the still body of his friend. Lightly, he shook Mitch's shoulder, but there was no response from the wizard. The night was loud as bugs and critters took over the forest. Lyra's soft sniffles and unsteady breaths were carried away with the wind.

Suddenly, a green spark danced in the air, just a few meters away from where Mitch's body laid. It swirled and spun, widening until a full portal was open.

A group of rangers and sentinels had begun storming out to help carry both Mitch and the horseman through the rift. It happened so quickly and smoothly, like an army of ants. Not a word was said, but they all had perfect formation as they carried Mitch and the horseman away. Lyra's gaze was stuck on the heroic wizard being carried away like a child.

Cedric turned to Lyra as she forced herself to her feet. Her long hair fell over her eyes. She was still for a moment, her hands clenched into fists. Finally, she snapped her head up and pushed onward through the portal, alone.

Cedric sighed, then slowly stood to follow.

Standing on the other side of the portal was the grand wizard, Gabriel, in his dark gray cloak. He observed the scene. His old eyes watched them as they transferred Mitch's body.

Captain Vansin instructed a few of his men to hunt down the horseman's steed. As the vampire turned back, he saw Gabriel standing there. His eyes stared at the blood that stained the ground where Mitchell was laying. The grand wizard looked angry but as Thaddeus analyzed, there seemed to also be guilt in his eyes. The captain couldn't remember the last time Gabriel showed any kind of emotion. It has been a very long time. Ever since their good friends Elijah and Linda Bettings died during battle many years ago. The vampire rubbed his mustache and wondered what the wizard was thinking, but as soon as Gabriel's eyes caught the captain looking at him, he pulled his hood over his head and walked back through the rift. Thaddeus took one more look at Sleepy Hollow, then disappeared into the glowing portal and left the scene where the tragedy took place.

Chapter 2

MODERN DAY

A crisp autumn breeze blows through the cracked open window. There is a faint knock on the door while a voice in the distance calls out, but Lyra barely notices while in her deep slumber.

"Fangs! Wake up!" Cedric's voice calls out louder. Lyra stirs in her sleep but turns over and dozes off once again. It takes another minute or two for her to crack an eye open. "Hello!? Girl, vampires have good hearing, so I know you can hear me!" he yells with a playful tone in his voice while knocking harder at the front door.

Lyra stares up at the ceiling examining the white paint above her. She sits up on her bed and notices a spider crawling on the light gray wood floor. She reluctantly pushes herself off the king-sized mattress and walks toward the arachnid. It starts to climb the black brick wall that her bed is in front of, and she slowly extends her finger, letting the spider crawl on her index.

She turns slowly, taking in her surroundings. Gliding around her bed, she analyzes her room. It has only been remodeled eight times…within the year. She painted the walls dark gray while the hickory wooden floorboards are a different shade of gray. The accent wall behind her bed pulls it all together. Her king bed frame is wrapped in a sleek black cushioned velvet fabric and was complemented with rhinestones. Her sheets are black silk with dark gray silk square decorative pillows. Her dressers and vanity, of course, are black with silver accents to match the bed. Redecorating helps take her mind off real life for a little while.

"C'mon little guy," Lyra whispers as she moves toward the balcony holding her hand up steadily. She pushes aside the dark blackout curtain revealing sheer white curtains. She quickly ties up the curtains to each side of the double doors and opens them carefully to not disturb the spider, who seems to be enjoying the ride. "There you go," she whispers as she guides her hand to the ivy branches that cover half of the walls outside her home.

"Aw, how touching, let's save some more critters before the captain rips our heads off because we are late to see him!" her partner shouts from the ground sarcastically as he watches her slowly help the spider.

Lyra smirks, "I'll be down in a moment." She covers herself with her silk black robe and walks back inside to get ready.

She strolls through her room, grabbing an all-black dagger from her elegant gigantic midnight tinted desk, twirling it in her hand as she looks for her attire for the day. The vampire decides to put some music on as she gets ready. The song

Coming Undone by Korn was always on top of her playlist for the past few months. With no eagerness to change quickly, Lyra goes to a small refrigerator and grabs a blood bag that had a small tag on it, showing the flavors. "I guess today will be pomegranate day." She pours the bag in a steel to-go cup, filled with ice, and moves towards the walk-in closet.

The vampire pulls out a black cropped jacket along with a black t-shirt and some black boots. Lyra examined herself in the coffin-shaped mirror that was mounted on the wall to see if she should have her jacket zipped up or not. The vampire left it open and once she was satisfied with her appearance, she opens her bedroom doors and walks through the hallway towards the grand staircase that leads down to the main entrance.

Lyra stops abruptly before her feet could reach the steps as she felt something staring at her from a nearby shelf. Her mood suddenly changes as the vampire turns her head. An old photo in a rusted gold frame captures an image of her, Cedric and Mitchell sitting in the middle of an old, wooden bookcase.

Memories flow through her head, remembering that day when the picture was taken. It was two years ago at the grand cemetery for the annual Spookish Carnival. The event celebrated the anniversary of their new world that saved thousands of creatures like them from the human realm.

The thought was bittersweet, with the recollection of the enjoyment they all had. Mason, Mitchell's brother, struck a deal that day with the captain that would allow him to walk free, all charges against him dropped. For the first time, Mitch was able to enjoy his time with him without his older brother getting into any trouble. It was also the first time she felt comfortable with her feelings towards the troubled wizard. Years of chasing and capturing Mason, it seemed like an odd connection between them started to form. With him being a free man and the feelings that she had been pushing aside for so long had now seemed okay to feel.

She caught her reflection in the glass. Somehow, she still looks unfamiliar to herself. Her thick hair is now shoulder length and wavy. Lyra tried to braid it, but only got just a couple done on one side. She told herself that she would finish the rest but did not come around to it.

The vampire stares at herself for another moment then proceeds forward, walking down the circular stairs to the ceiling high double doors.

She reaches to undo the locks and as soon as she turns the knobs, they burst open with her partner's forceful hands.

"When somebody says that they'll be down in a moment, they don't mean almost an hour later!" Cedric is always on time for everything. If he is not ten minutes early, then he considers himself late.

She takes amusement knowing that she irritates the wolf from her being the opposite. She smirks, watching him freak out as they are late to see her father at the station. "Ok wolf boy, relax, we'll just tell the captain that there was a mix up with the blood bags that I got and had to exchange the years on them."

Cedric shakes his head, "We blame them too much already. Your father is going to be more serious with the blood bank because that's a huge deal!"

She rolls her eyes and agrees, "Fine, then I'll just tell him that I overslept again. Happy?"

He smiles, satisfied enough, "Good, because that's actually more believable than getting the wrong aged blood or any other excuses you had running through your thick head."

The vampire was impressed with Cedric's humor as she gave his shoulder a light shove. They walk down the few steps from the porch towards his car. She slides her fingertips along the hood of the vehicle towards the door handle. "Another muscle car? I'm a little thrown off by the color choice though. I could've sworn werewolves didn't like the color silver."

While unlocking the door, he looks up at her and sees a wide grin that spreads across her face. "You're such a pain in the ass, Fangs." He rolls his eyes at her as he tries not to encourage her by laughing.

They get into the car and drive off through the narrow roads, letting their presence be known by the engine roar. Lyra looks out the window towards the overcast sky, following each tree that they passed with her eyes, admiring their leaf's change to orange and red. Seeing the mountains and waterfalls during their trip to the city was Lyra's reason for moving out there. The scenery is peaceful, and it calms her.

However, no matter how beautiful the drive is, she keeps

thinking back to the photo from earlier. It is difficult not to think about events that happened almost a year ago. She cannot believe it has almost been a year since the tragedy of Mitch's death. Maybe if he had been more serious, or paid attention, or if she paid attention. She lets herself become distracted about the guilt that she has to live with forever. Her mind tortures her with the repeating thoughts of the tragic accident with Mitchell and how she has not heard from his brother ever since the funeral. *Was Mason angry that his brother died on my watch? Was he disgusted with me that I let him down because I was too distracted by a human instead of the mission at hand?* Her thoughts keep asking the same questions, but she cannot find an answer.

"Everything okay?" A voice pulls Lyra from her own mind as she looks over and sees Cedric staring at her, waiting for an answer.

"Yeah, sorry, I'm fine," she mumbles, slightly embarrassed that he caught her lost in thought. Lyra turns her attention to a new distraction, her black ripped pants, perfect for rubbing her fingers through the strings in one of the knee holes. The car falls silent again, so Cedric reaches for the radio to play something other than the memories that he knew were racing through her mind. The anniversary is tomorrow, and it is settling in their minds.

Their vehicle re-emerges from a short tunnel formed by the thick leafless trees along the pathway as they pull up to a set of large steel gates protecting Hexington Falls.

Cedric parks along the side by one of the giant limestone statues of the courageous witches and wizards that had sacrificed themselves to create a world for their kind to flourish. The statues sit outside the city to be seen by everyone who visits. Behind the seven statues, there emerges a giant stone wall, circling the city and keeping all the unwanted creatures from the forest out of their home.

Lyra and Cedric both step out of the vehicle and walk through the gate, passing a few rangers that eye them cautiously. As the two enter, the energy changes drastically. Cedric, being raised in London, felt right at home in the city, almost oblivious to the change in the air. "Ahh, I love the busy streets of this town!"

Lyra glances at him and lets the moment be enjoyable, giving him a soft smile. Looking around the town taking everything in with an *at home* feeling, Lyra could not disagree. "Yeah, it definitely takes my mind off things, you know- this energy."

She too glances around, but not like the wonder and awe that glistens in Cedric's eyes. "Everyone has it, everything here has it," Cedric finishes.

The two presses on as silence starts to fall again. "Why don't you just move back here inside the walls? It's closer to work and everyone is basically here?" he asks, already knowing the answer.

The vampire pushes on, eyes snapping forward on the path, blocking out any bit of *awe* there was to find. "We're late, aren't we?"

Cedric stops walking, "I miss him too."

Lyra's feet's stick to the ground. She cannot find the power to move, mind stuck on Cedric's words and all that they carry. The vampire cannot help but feel the guilt coursing through her body. She makes a quick glance toward Cedric and nods at him, along with a fake smile then proceeds to make their way to the station.

Cedric knows he is not going to get anywhere with that conversation and jumps topics, understandingly, "Now the only Bettings bloodline we have left is the pain in the ass."

She lets out a chuckle but then, almost immediately, any hint of joy in the woman was gone in a glimpse. She just could not find the excuse to be happy when a wizard, a friend, was still gone. That is unacceptable to her. Mitch was someone everyone looked up to. He always put others first and had a positive attitude, no matter the problem or the risk. His brother, Mason, on the other hand, was the opposite. Mason was always getting into trouble growing up and never took his wizard schooling seriously. When everyone looks at him, they only see a troublemaker while Lyra sees something else. Even though there were many times she had to be the one to bring him into custody, there is always a spark between them that she cannot shake.

As Lyra and Cedric walk along the cobblestone road and through the crowded town, they arrive at the police station. Just outside there is a dark gray, three-tier, concrete fountain that sits dried up and stuffed with a couple dozen jack-o-lanterns that are laying inside each tier as well as the floor surrounding it. Everyone that comes from out of town makes sure they get their pictures taken with it when they are here. Behind the fountain is a large five-story building with red brick walls and thick bronze doors.

Seems like a regular day at the office with rangers moving around and appearing to work diligently. Rangers are made up of many different creatures dedicated to keeping the city of Hexington Falls safe. They all sport a dark gray hooded poncho that draped just above their black utility belts. Under, they had on their navy jumpsuits and black combat boots. An electrical pack is strapped tightly onto the backs, made specifically for protection by the great Doctor. To an unfamiliar eye it may come off as if it could explode at any moment, with all the wires and batteries sticking out. However, everything that the doctor makes is flawless, so far. The small pack has a cord that connects to a blaster that is typically placed in a holster that is at the hip. In attack mode, the weapon shoots out blue electric rounds, set to stun any unlucky target, unless of course the rounds are switched out by something more deadly. Although uncommon, it was not unheard of for the rangers to twist the barrel and exchange stun rounds for something more permanent with a red glow to them.

Cedric pushes the doors open. "After you, boss lady." He adds in a bow to compliment his performance and to put a smile on Lyra's face before starting their shift.

"Gracias," she replies with a playful salute as she strides through the open door.

"Good evening Ms. Vansin," a voice chimes from behind the desk as the pair enter the lobby of the building. Lyra spots a young lady wearing a black Metallica t-shirt sitting down behind a computer. Her gray beanie has long wavy copper hair flowing out from underneath it and down her back. Upon her olive-colored skin are patches of dark green reptilian scales on her body that almost look like tattoos. Her hazel eyes could draw in any creature that may glance her way with her large circular glasses that sat on her button nose.

"Oh, hello Samara," the vampire replies with a quick hand wave as she and Cedric continue past the glowing receptionist and onward toward the elevator. Cedric gives a quick nod in Samara's direction as he usually gets tongue tied trying to speak to the half reptile. She gives a shy smile and looks down quickly at her computer pretending to work but slowly glances up to look back at him as the two enter the elevator.

The elevator doors close and without missing a beat, Cedric fills the silence, "Good lord, I'm glad the first thing I see when we walk in is Samara Tillia! She's so fine with her smile and those gorgeous eyes." He seems lost in the void, eyes glistening while spacing out at the thought of his interest in the half human reptile.

Lyra smiles and pushes Cedric's arm playfully. "I don't know why you don't just ask her out already. I notice how *both* of you look at each other."

Cedric's eyes shift to Lyra, taking him out of his dream

and back to the harsh reality. "Maybe one day I will. When the time is right, you know?" He begins rubbing the back of his neck. "Also.... I want to make sure that she's not the type that... eats her partners."

Lyra rolls her eyes as Cedric's mind drifts off once more, but with the thought of him being eaten. "I just think that could be a deal breaker for me."

Ding! The elevator doors open. On the other side is a tall man standing there, waiting for them. He towers over them in his black knitted sweater that has small metal buckles on the right side keeping it buttoned up. His skin is faded green with a red accent cybernetic arm attaching to his large muscular body. He has many scars along his whole body that slither under his clothes and hairline.

Cedric, releases a wide smile, jumps out of the elevator to greet the man with excitement, "Frankie! What's up man! Or men?" He jokes with him, eyeing the giant scars on his body from multiple dead bodies that it took to create him.

"Hi friends," Frankie greets them with a deep voice. The monster seemed pleased to see them with a wide smile. Frankie escorts Lyra and Cedric to the captain's office. "The doctor said to find you and let you know your dad needs you."

Cedric slowly turns his head towards Lyra and waits for her to finally look his way, which does not take long. Cedric immediately shoots her a scowl. The vampire gives him a light innocent shrug with an awkward smile and continues following the bulky lab creature.

The trio make their way to the end of the hallway and enter a large office space filled with cubicles and creatures working. Frankie extends his cybernetic arm forward like a security detail. "I heard that captain has been waiting for you two. Doctor feels like it could be some good news because he looks a little, you know, less grumpy than normal." He smiles at them as they reach the captain's door.

Lyra hears a familiar voice behind her, "Hey Lyra, you got a second?" She turns her head to see a man striding up to her while rolling up the sleeves of his dark blue button up shirt. It's Hunter Jackson, another vampire she met a few months ago that, like her, looks to be in his late twenties. Unlike her, Hunter was turned four years ago by an illegal vampire coven in Savannah, Georgia. These covens were all over the human world and it was the job of teams, like the Nocturnal Squad, to take them down when discovered.

The fanged creature was tall and had blonde curly hair. Hunter always dresses as if he was a cool college professor with a slightly chewed pencil stored behind his ear and two top buttons of his shirt unbuttoned. Even though they had spent some quality time together, Lyra honestly did not know too much about the young-looking vampire, besides the fact that he was a cop during his human life and that he had a cute southern accent. The dates that they had gone on, Lyra's mind was always simply somewhere else. Hunter is a damn good ranger, top of his class at the academy, but after the year she had, it is hard for her to come around romantically, even though she thought he was extremely attractive.

"Hey, I was trying to meet up with you sooner, but I should've known better than to think *you* would be on time!" He laughs with his confident charming grin, revealing his fangs. Lyra cannot help but blush at the sight of his gorgeous smile and sparkling ocean eyes. She begins to tuck her hair behind her ear but immediately stops, trying not to give out the wrong signal.

Hunter steps in front of her, knowing how she may try to avoid any uncomfortable conversation. "Look, I know I've been pushing and not letting up, but I was wondering if you would like to go out for a late-night dinner again sometime? Last time was enchanting and I know a nice spot in Eerie Oaks."

Lyra just stares at him for a moment to think about the idea of another date. She knows Hunter wants to be something more than just friends going out to dinner. He's a nice guy that any girl would be fortunate to be with, but she regretfully does not feel that she is *there* just yet. "Their steaks are to die for," he tosses in.

"Hunter, that sounds great, but I'm not ready for someone to just come in and be my prince charming and do all those fancy things couples are supposed to do…. right now. I just want to focus more on my job for now." Her body slouches a little after giving him the news, but knows it is right, well, for now at least.

"Yeah, she's more of a, 'oh let's see if we can find a dead body by the lake and bask in the fumes of the decaying flesh with a nice pumpkin spice latte', kinda gal," Cedric interrupts sarcastically, while lightly bumping into the two's conversation and giving Lyra a hand gesture to hurry the convocation up. She shoots her partner a scowl while trying not to laugh.

Hunter grabs her hand gently, "Look, I get it. There's no rush. We have an eternity to figure something out." He loosens his grip on her hand while giving one last smirk then walks back to his desk.

Lyras head rolls towards Frank and Cedric while giving her partner a look for the interruption. "Hazelnut," she states.

"What?" Cedric asked, confused.

"Hazelnut latte, not pumpkin," she corrects him.

Cedric breaks into his devilish grin followed by an evil laugh, "Well, *Buddy* apparently has an eternity to figure that out. I wonder if you would have said *No* to Mason."

"Really? You think I wouldn't?" Lyra shoots back along with daggers in her eyes.

"Hey, it's not me you need to convince. The look on your face every time you come across him, whether it's on the job or not. These eyes see all," Cedric presses on.

Lyra denies his allegations, "I just enjoy easy cases, that is all."

He scoffs, "Easy!? The only people who could catch him were you and Mitch. Mitchell was his brother so that gave him an edge, but you on the other hand..." Cedric lingers, not needing to say more.

"What? You think he just lets me catch him? Why He

would he do something so stupid like that?"

He looks at her with a smirk, waiting for her to come up with the answer herself. "Because he probably fancies you too. He used to leave you a petal of a flower every time he gave you the slip. Not just any kind of flower peddle either. But a sunflower! Your favorite, if I'm not mistaken."

She raised an eyebrow at him, "Look, I tried reaching out to Mason, but he left without a word. If he really had feelings for me, then he would have let me in after his brother died and I get it. It's about to hit a year and we still haven't heard from him. He clearly doesn't fancy me."

"But what if he does?" Cedric argues back, "And then what if he sees you with *college-boy* over there?"

"Well, then he sees me. He's a big boy and should know I'm not going to wait for anyone, so if another guy is interested in me…. then he knows what's up!" Her confidence crashes at the end of her power speech.

Cedric is caught off guard with her attitude as he tries not to laugh, "He knows what's up? Who are you!?"

Lyra rolls her eyes as they are interrupted by Frankie who is awkwardly standing in the middle of the two, "Sorry friends, but the captain has a meeting soon and wants to see you before."

They apologize and walk towards the office. Lyra lightly knocks then proceeds to open the door. "You wanted to see us, Captain?"

"Ah, yes come in," The captain greets them, standing by the window looking out at the other buildings and the pesquet's parrots flying around. "Cedric, if you don't mind, I would like to speak with my daughter for a moment alone."

The wolf glances at Lyra, confused, "You got it Captain." He gives his partner a quick wave then leaves, closing the double doors behind him.

"Please, have a seat," her father insists, while striding across the room to grab a folder off a wooden bookcase.

Lyra eyes him curiously. She cannot help but wonder what her father wants to talk about. The vampire walks toward her father's broad oak desk and sits, putting her cup on a gold-plated coaster next to some loose paperwork scattered on the dark wood. "Is everything okay? I was getting a *good news* type of energy walking into work," she comments with uncertainty.

"Oh, but of course. That is why I've summoned you here," Her father says with a smooth, but low calm voice.

Thaddeus lightly tosses the file on his desk in his daughter's direction. Lyra looks up at her father, then at the red manila folder. She reaches out for it and does not hesitate to open it.

The captain stands tall, waiting, as his daughter's eyes scan the file. Finally, she looks up at him with her curiosity gone and replaced with furrowed eyebrows as Lyra exclaims, "You're retiring? After all these years, why? What are you going to do? Who's going to take over?" She rambles off a series of questions, unsure of what she wants answered first, or if she really wants all those questions answered.

The captain gives her a smirk, "This has been on my mind for years, but the timing never seemed right." He grabs her hand and continues, "For centuries, I've been doing this, protecting the citizens' thing, and keeping the peace. I was there, in the beginning and earned my way up the ranks." He pauses, eyes locked on a silver sword sitting in an elegant glass case on top of his bookshelf. "I fought in the vampires-werewolf war then helped with the treaty to end the violence." Thaddeus paces the floor then his eyes return to Lyra's. His smile grows wider as he remembers his first moments with her. "But with all of my accomplishments the one that shines above it all is the day I met you," he says as his eyes glaze over as if lost in thought.

The captain shakes his head and walks back to the window, looking out as he remembers *that day* perfectly. Lyra walks back to her seat as he reveals where his mind had wondered to, "I used to go to the human realm to collect blood for our world. We needed the blood to keep other vampires from wanting to escape to the human world themselves. But I digress, on one of my trips I was in Mexico for a supply run until I found myself within range of a beast that I had been chasing for quite some time." The captain stops. He takes a sip of his tea before continuing. "It led me to your home… and that, my dear, is where I met your birth mother." He grabs the small teacup off the small table near him and takes a sip, "When I saw you, you were resting without a care in all the world. She told me that you were sick, and the doctors couldn't do anything." The captain continues telling the story as if it all happened yesterday.

"What the hell is going on here?" a woman exclaimed. Thaddeus slowly turned around to the voice that broke through his attack mode. There was blood splattered around the small house. He knew that it could not have looked good as he had slowly turned around, body still tense, and was ready to fight if necessary. With just one look at the beautiful, but distraught woman, his muscles relaxed, and he could feel a sense of relief. The young woman did a quick assessment of the scene.

Little Lyra turned over in her sleep. The woman ran to her daughter's bed to check on her, but she was knocked out. Elizabeth wiped a tear and turned back to the man, "Thank you for saving my daughter! I really did not mean to leave her alone for so long but, I-I had to work, I just," She pinched the bridge of her nose and closed her eyes. The woman looked exhausted, with bags under her eyes. She sighed, "Bills just are, uh, catching up. I uh, work is-it's taking more time than usual, I just... Día de los Muertos is a big holiday for selling my items and I don't have someone to watch her-"

"No need to thank me or explain. This creature would have attacked if you were here or not and no offense, but I'm not sure you could have done much. I'm just glad I could do my part."

Elizabeth's eyes began to water, thankful that this hero really understood. He could see all this woman carried, but also, he felt a deep feeling toward her. The hero stepped toward her and pulled the small woman in for a hug. She wrapped her arms around him and let her weight fall into him. He could feel her frame tremble in his arms as she let out soft cries of all that she burdened with and the idea of what could have happened to her baby.

The vampire pulled back to look into her eyes. He gave her a soft smile as he wiped the tear stains from her cheeks. "It's okay," he said, so calm, yet confident.

Their faces were inches from each other. Her hands were still wrapped around his neck and his on her waist. That night he decided to bring the blood back to his home, then take time off to stay in Mexico for a little. His short stay turned into weeks then months and then years. Time had flown by as he watched over little Lyra and her mom.

On one fateful morning, he decided to tell Elizabeth the truth about vampires and the rules that came along with it. He stepped into their kitchen where Elizabeth swayed as she hummed a soft tune over the beginning of breakfast. She spun around upon hearing her lover, "Good morning!" Her smile fell as she could tell something was wrong. "What is it?"

Thaddeus pulls out a seat at the kitchen table, "I have to tell you something."

As the couple sat across from one another, he explained the rules of vampires when it came to love with another species. If a vampire falls in love with a human and they decide to marry, the human must turn into a vampire or the vampire dies when the human does, but only if it's natural causes. The ceremony was to be a blood pact and the magic in the vampire blood would connect them. This blood bond would be able to sense the death and if the vampire lives or dies.

The woman was heartbroken as she heard the curse of vampires. He did not want to die, but she did not want to live forever, no matter how much she loved him. Even if she would be able to use this curse to save Lyra's life from her sickness. With a heavy heart, Elizabeth decided that it would be best if they were apart so that he did not have to choose or live with regret.

A couple of days later, back in Hexington Falls, Thaddeus heard over the radio that Manzanillo, Mexico got hit with a deadly hurricane. He rushed as fast as he could to see if Elizabeth and her daughter were safe.

As he got to their neighborhood, he saw what tragedy had taken place. He rushed to find them but had no luck. Thaddeus heard noises, but when he went to move the debris out of the way, he found unfamiliar victims of the storm. The vampire was devastated. His heart was pounding hard as he was trying to put his anger over his fear. After searching for hours, he could not find them. All hope was lost. He thought about Elizabeth and how much he wanted to see her again.

"No, I will not give up," he said under his breath. He thought about them both and knew he needed to focus. It took a moment to collect himself, but as he closed his eyes, he pictured both Lyra and Elizabeth. He focused on their smiles and his love for the both of them.

As his heart calmed, he heard a familiar voice, "There!"

A few houses down, Thaddeus found them. They were trapped under a bunch of rubble, so he used his strength to remove it all out of the way. The vampire pulled off what seemed to be part of the roof and that's when he saw Elizabeth's still body.

The same soft skinned frame he once held on to was lifeless on the floor next to Lyra. He took her hand into his. As soon as he did, his heart shattered. A sharp pain shot through his own chest as he became dizzy and foggy headed as if dreaming. His legs shook and his stomach dropped as the nausea settled in.

The sun beat down on the accident. Despite a thick coat used for protection, the sun was still starting to burn the heart-broken vampire. He was running out of time.

"Papa, I'm scared. Will it hurt to die?" A weak voice was heard next to him. Lyra's eyes were dozing off as the vampire could focus in and heard her heart beating slower and slower.

Thaddeus moved closer to her, "No, because death won't last long if you drink some of my blood." He holds her against his chest. "Wouldn't you like to live life to its fullest? Live forever? With me?"

She nodded her little head that felt so heavy as death was coming for her. Until she told him, "Yes."

Captain Vansin looks over at his beautiful, adopted daughter, "And the one who will replace me when I retire will be you. If you choose to accept it."

Lyra is shocked and at a loss for words. "Oh, wow I-I don't know what to say." So many thoughts flood her mind, then suddenly, only one thought remains. "What about my team? I can't just get up and leave like that," she says, thinking that they have not fully healed from the devastation of last year's incident.

"Look, I'm not leaving today. I'm giving you time to bring Cedric to your level and train the recruit before having you promoted," the captain informs her, putting her mind at ease.

Her heart begins to ease as her own panic settles until she finally processes her father's words. "A new recruit?"

"Ah, yes I was just about to get to that," the captain replied. The news of the newest recruit is overshadowed by his surprise retirement announcement. "We have extended our search for a suitable candidate to the town of Hickory Lakes and found a promising young man. With a little push, he can be a fine asset to your squadron. You will be able to find him in the lab right now with Dr. Franklin Stein, working on some new tech for the lad. Also, Lyra, take your time with your decision. You have plenty of time."

Lyra shakes the captain's hand and with a smile, she thanks him for everything. She walks out of his office and heads to the lab. Cedric sees her leaving and says goodbye to Frankie so he can catch up with her. "Hey, so what happened? Is everything ok?" He asks while looking for an answer and trying to match her speed.

"Yeah, I mean--" She pauses and comes to a sudden halt. With all the information she just received, Lyra finds the words.

"He wants to promote me to captain and be his replacement," she sums it up quickly, as it takes Cedric longer to process than her to blurt out.

"C'mon, I know you said yes.... did you just say yes?" he mumbles out, still trying to wrap his head around the idea.

Lyra begins to walk again while shaking her head, "I don't know what I want at this moment, but he did tell me that we got a new guy joining us, so we are on our way to meet him."

Cedric still stands there, dumbfounded at the twist of a new recruit, "wow uh... ok cool um... yeah, alright then."

Chapter 3

The room is dark. An unknown whisper fills the stale air. Etta's eyes flutter open and she suddenly sits up on her bed. "Hello?" She looks around the barren gray room to see if anyone was with her. She does not see anyone except for the dancing shadows on the single wardrobe in the corner of the room cast by the moon through a small window. Inside the wardrobe were three sets of beige scrubs. How she despised the color beige after months of the same color. *I can't believe it has almost been a year since Mitch's death*, she sadly thought to herself. The witch continued scanning around the room and brought her knees to her chest and wrapped her arms around them. She began taking a mental note of her limited belongings, ugly beige loafers, ugly brown wooden table, and chair with a single notebook (pens and pencils need to be checked out and returned), and a knee length beige robe.

A whisper speaks in her ear. "No, I can't," she replies to the mysterious voice. "I already told you it's impossible... I can't." Etta's voice cracks as she buries her head in her knees. The whispers surround her bedroom and get louder. "Ok, I'll do it!" she agrees while lifting her head to the unknown voice.

Slowly shifting her body to the edge of the bed, she puts her feet on the cold stone floor. Lifting her pillow, the witch grabs a wooden wand that was hidden. Etta tried casting a spell but the tech that was placed on her wrist kept her from using her magic. The wooden wand she made was to help channel her powers due to the dampener.

Ugh, this feels like starting to learn how to do magic all over again, she thought to herself. As a more advanced witch, she isn't used to speaking out spells that she was trying to do. All she had to do was think of what she wanted and do it. With the tech on her arm, it made her start all over from the beginning. Etta cast a spell as quietly as she could "Vivamos lux invisibilis!" A blue light orb appeared but then vanished. She tried a few more times until it held. Struggling to keep it, Etta tried to see what she needed. Grabbing the ugly beige robe from her wardrobe, she collects the few supplies she was able to acquire from underneath her mattress and swings her bag over her shoulder.

A corner of a book peaked out from under her bed. The title read "Voodoo". The witch remembered when she took this book. It was the same day that the grand wizard ordered for her magic to be bound by the device that was now attached to her arm. That night, she snuck out of her room and made her way down to the library to look for answers that would help bring her husband back to life. Every book she read prior was too risky or at least difficult to achieve. Sneaking around was an easy task after doing it a few times, but that night she took too long and got caught. The witch stumbled across the book and refused to have it taken away, so she fought to distract them from seeing it in her possession. A few witches and wizards got hurt, but in her mind, it was worth it. Until they stopped her from using her powers anymore, that is.

Etta turns toward the door knowing that it will be locked but the voice insists for her to still try. "They lock my door now, so I don't try to leave again," she informed the mysterious voice. It whispers louder as it continues to convince her to try, but she wasn't going to get her hopes up because escaping her room was just the first step. "If I could leave this room, I still would have to slip through all the guards that are patrolling the castle and make my way to the vault to steal the heart of mare which would be heavily guarded. It's impossible!" she explained. The voice appears again, ordering her to open the door and this time, she gives in. "Okay, I'll try it!"

Etta reaches for the doorknob, extending her fingertips. As her hand grips the handle, it began turning. She expected it to stop, however it did not. The witch was surprised that they forgot to lock her door today of all days. The wooden door creaked open, and she peaks her head out, looking around to see if there were sentinels guarding the halls near her room. Etta moves quietly along the walls of the castle, being discreet as she casts the orb to light her path. Every five steps, she casts the orb to help her see until it dies out.

Etta is dedicated, concentrating her magic through the wooden wand she used as a substitute for her energy wand. The grand wizard underestimated the witch, but she was smart and very gifted in her magic. She ended up making her own wand from the furniture in her room.

She makes her way to the vault where the dark and dangerous artifacts were held. Surprisingly, the halls were all empty. Etta was surprised once more that there wasn't anyone patrolling the floor where the vault was. The witch picks the lock to the thick steel door and unlocks it. The vault makes a loud thud sound as it unlocks. She slowly opens it and there it is. Towards the end on top of a table alone is the stone called the Heart of Mare.

"This is it! This is the creation of all things wicked. Powered by fear of others to create creatures people fear most!" she whispered, trying to contain her excitement. The witch takes a moment to soak it all in. The heart of mare hasn't been seen in decades. It was the shape of a heart with an amber color to it. The monster known as a mare haunted people, giving them horrible dreams until it was killed. The body became ashes, but the heart turned into an unbreakable stone that if activated, along with enough fear feeding it, the dark artifact would be able to create supernatural beings that people believed in.

A couple of voices in the distance started to form and only got louder as they got closer. Etta turns and quickly leaves the vault. The distant voices grow even louder as shadows start to appear from the corner. She finds a door a few feet away from her and dashes through. The witch attempts casting an orb again and the light quickly lit up the room, showing her a staircase.

Walking down the steps, the mysterious voice returns. "Stop it! If I can't think then I won't be able to do what I must do!" she aggressively replies. The whispers stop immediately. Step by step, she walks down the narrow staircase until she reaches the bottom. As she makes it to the end, Etta finds another door with a little window in the middle of it. She peeks through the glass to see if anyone is around.

"There's somebody out there by the exit," Etta informs the voice. She waits a moment to get a reply but nothing. "Are you still there?" she asks, but still no answer. She grows frustrated with how when she wants the voice to speak to her, it doesn't. The witch starts to feel as if she was going crazy. Maybe the voices were not real. That it was all created in her head due to the trauma that happened in the past.

"KILL HIM!" the voice aggressively whispers, demanding her to murder the man who didn't pose a threat.

"What!? No! I can't do that! He's a friend! That's Danny!" she argues back, while slightly starting to panic. Etta knows that she must continue and knows that she must think of something quick before people realize that she's missing.

"You won't have another shot at saving your husband if you are caught again," the voice explains.

Etta studies those words in her head as she looks back up at her friend that was standing on the other side of the door. She wipes the sweat off her face as her heart starts to race. The witch grips the wooden wand that she's holding and slowly walks into the hall. Etta moves behind Danny and raises her wand at him. For a moment, she hesitates. She doesn't understand how everything came to this point. Everything used to be different, better to be exact. Everyone she used to trust and be friends with suddenly backed away from her. They all started to think that she was going mad. That she needed help, but nobody understood. No one tried to understand. Out of nowhere, she became an outcast. She felt betrayed. With all her thoughts flooding through her mind, with all the pain and anger she was feeling, she raises her arm and uses the thick metal armband to knock her wizard friend unconscious. He began to fall to the floor and just before his head could hit the ground, Etta quickly catches him and places his head gently on the floor.

"Let's go!" she tells the voice, pulling her hood over her head as she starts to run out of the castle. Etta escapes through the open field toward the forest that surrounds their community. The full moon is shining yellow as she makes her way to the trees. Making her way up a hill, she looks back at the castle, thinking about her past and the friends she's leaving behind. For a moment, she starts to feel sad at what happened but then turns toward the next town, Hexington Falls, and starts imagining her future. Everything can be fixed.

"I can make things go back to how they were. Nobody understands yet, but just wait, they will," she tries to convince herself. Etta puts her hand on her leather bag to make sure everything was safe, and then continues.

As she sprints through the forest, Etta is also being wary of the creatures that she knows live within. Along with bears, moose and wild boars, there are other beasts like basilisks, chupacabras and even wendigos that roam around the scene.

Etta moves through the trees in her path and suddenly slips down a muddy slope. She falls and lands on her back. On the ground, she turns her head to see her satchel a few feet away from her. Etta turns her body over and starts to lift herself back up. She gets up on one knee and leans over to reach her bag. Above her, she hears leaves rustling. Etta lifts her head up and with quick instinct reflexes, jerks her body back out of the way just as a giant, man-eating plant snaps down at her. Quickly getting up to her feet, she pulls out her wand from her waist and points it toward the creature and blasts a burst of flame from the tip to burn it. The flame ended up being small, but it was all she needed. The monstrous plant gave a loud wail and retracted back into the bushes where it came from.

"I thought those things got destroyed in one of the wars years ago," Etta mumbles to herself. Looking around her surroundings to make sure no other surprises occur, she resumes her quest. "Are you still there?" Etta calls out, not hearing from it since she crossed the walls from her town.

"Continue," the low voice answers.

Getting back on the path towards Hexington Falls, the witch hears howling nearby. "Oh no! Wolves!" She tries not to draw any attention to herself. Etta picks up the pace but then she stops in her tracks and looks over her shoulder. Staring back at her with their yellow eyes is a pack of werewolves. "I forgot how big they looked when they're in this form," she whispers while slowly backing away and sliding her hand to her wand just in case. The large hairy beasts are just standing there as if they are trying to see Etta's next move. Standing up on their two back legs and growling like they were waiting to attack her, but that's all that had happened. Etta gets the idea that they may be occupied by something else and just wants to make sure she's not there to interrupt them. The one in the middle seemed to be the one in charge and he just stares at her with his glowing yellow eyes and a scar on his left side of his face. The witch was glad that she's not their priority right now. Etta raises both hands to show that she does not have a weapon and is not there to interfere in whatever they were doing. This seems to satisfy them as slowly, one by one, they begin to disappear into the night.

Walking as fast as she possibly could without making too much noise, she was finally out of the deep forest. Etta arrives at the gates of Hexington Falls. Looking through the thick bars, she begins thinking of a way to get in and go unnoticed through the town to the other side. Her mission was to reach The Cave of Passage where there was a portal to the human realm.

Brainstorming ideas through her head, the voice returns whispering into her ear, "open the gates of the wicked."

"What? What do you mean?"

"The wicked that are being held captive beneath the surface."

Etta's eyes widen as she starts to understand what the voice meant. A flickering light flashes a wooden sign that reads Downcast Prison. "That might just work!" she says with hope.

The witch slips through the city undetected. With people walking around the streets, Etta had to move whichever way was clear, even if it made the route longer. She found herself cutting through a clothing shop "Broom Closet? Time to get out of these horrible clothes."

The shop is a popular clothing store that every city has. It has five floors with a dark wood interior. Each floor is sorted for every being living within Hexington Falls. The center of the store had an open layout, so you were able to look up at all the levels. Hanging from the ceiling is a giant elegant chandelier made of antlers that shines brighter than all the other lights inside the store.

Etta makes her way to the third floor where the human-like sizes are. She angles her head down, so she won't be recognized by anyone. Luckily for her, the store isn't really that busy. A few wizards casually walk towards where she stood, so she darts inside the dressing rooms. The witch finds a few outfits, but only one was her size. "Black jeans and gray long sleeve shirt? Going from one bland color to the next." She rolls her eyes when she sees the waist high hooded gray cloak that ended up matching her attire. "Not what I would have picked but no time to style it up. Definitely better than beige." After grabbing black boots from the rack just outside of the fitting room, the witch gets out back on the streets to continue her task.

Sneaking through the alley, she makes her way to an open space with an iron opening on the ground surrounded by concrete. Etta scans her surroundings to see if anyone is patrolling the area. When she felt that it was safe, she proceeded. Rushing to the door, Etta unlocks the hatch and lifts the giant metal bar open with difficulty. She climbs down the ladder and sneaks down the spiral staircase until she reaches the holding chambers. A ranger stood guard in front of a cell block, so she knocks him out the same way with Danny. Three more rangers are inside patrolling the area so she must quickly knock them out before they notice her and sound the alarm, which would blow her mission before it began.

Wandering from level to level, she looks for the perfect decoy for her to get through the city unspotted. The voice gave Etta options, but she rejected the ideas. "No not this one, I don't see an evil clown helping at all unless I wanted someone to lose sleep at night. Don't even say anything about that giant worm because that's just disgusting!"

She continues her search. "This one! This one will get it done!" There was no doubt in her mind, especially with time not being on her side. Etta stands back as she smashes the electric keypad to unlock the cell. The alarm begins to ring as it slowly starts to open. She began to run out, leaving all the doors open for the beast to go through. As she gets to the main entrance, she hears a loud gurgling and wet roar closing in behind her. Was this a mistake? If it is, Etta can't afford to second guess it.

Chapter 4

Walking into the elevator and taking it down to the basement where Dr. Stein's lab is, Lyra and Cedric talk about the recruit.

"So, we got a rook huh?" Cedric asked, looking at his partner. "Do you know what type of species?"

"Uh no, I didn't ask... My mind was kinda all over the place back there," Lyra replied, happy for her father but at the same time she feels that her place is on the field and not stuck in the office.

Cedric nods as he sees the concern on her face. He has been working with her for about six years now, so he had an idea of what she was thinking at times. "Whatever you choose, I will always have your back, Fangs."

The vampire appreciates his loyalty. After all the missions they've gone on, he is one of the reasons she loves doing what she does. She hopes to continue this gig in the future and hopes that the captain has a change of heart about leaving.

Arriving at the laboratory, they walk out to look for the

doctor and the recruit. Hearing noises on the other side behind a rack of old equipment, they see Franklin standing by a hospital bed. The whole room looks like a cluttered mess but to the doctor, it was an organized mess. He used to have his own building, miles away from the city where he could do all of his experiments in peace but there were too many uninvited guests who tried to take many of the doctor's weaponized inventions.

"Oh, hello! Captain Vansin informed me that you two will be coming by," the doctor welcomed. "I will be right with you shortly."

Both Lyra and Cedric trade glances, wondering where the recruit was. Someone who will be joining their squadron should have some form of tactical training and agility, but the only person they saw was just the doctor. Frankie walks in from behind to give his creator a car battery that he requested. Is the recruit Frankie? The doctor would never allow him to go out there on the field. Frankie was the doctor's first creation. The large monster was like a son he never had. The doctor even replaced parts of himself with cybernetics over the years because he wanted to make sure that there was always someone there to protect Frankie. He didn't trust anyone with that task. He has what looks like a fishbowl over his head filled with a liquid to keep himself preserved. At this point, the doctor is more of a machine than a man.

"Hey, uh doc? I thought we were meeting a new guy?" Cedric asked, confused. "Frankie.... Are you--" right before Cedric could finish his question, out of thin air, a man in a wired tech suit that covered him from head to toe, appears right in front of the wolf.

"I'm Liam!" the strange man says in a deep creepy voice the second he shows, introducing himself. He pops up with the wires around his suit malfunctioning, sparks making a zapping sound. He looked like he was glitching.

"What the hell!" Cedric screams, startled by Liam's random presence.

"Oh man, my bad," Liam quickly reacts while twitching due to the wires slightly shocking him, assuring that he's friendly. "In my head, that whole intro went differently. Thought it would have been a cool superhero intro," he added with his hands on his waist along with an awkward nodding. He looks back towards the doctor, amazed at the suit's technology. "This bad boy is awesome, doc! But can we make it a little less…Shockey?"

"Glad you approve and no worries. All I have to do is make some minor adjustments and it should be ready to go," the doctor replies. Frankie helps Liam take off the gear as the doctor takes one last look, evaluating his work. "But once it's complete, anything you wear will be able to cloak along with your body, matching your skin's complexion."

Liam turns back to Lyra and Cedric to shake their hands. "Anyways, my name is Liam, Liam Santos."

"So... Your skill is that you can turn invisible? Interesting," Lyra was impressed. "The *Invisible-Guy*!"

"Actually, I don't turn invisible. I just am," Liam

responds as he takes off the gray mask that had been covering his head, revealing his unseen face. "Also, the word *guy* makes it seem like I'm not that important and that I will be killed off during the first act so let's change it to *man,* ok?" he adds while using his fingers as air quotes.

"Mr. Santos' body seems to be in a permanent cloaking state," Dr. Stein interrupts, explaining the rookie's condition. "But my invention will be able to have his clothing match his skin and camouflage, so he won't have to worry about the exposure of his modesty."

"Wait, so all this time until now, you had to be naked to be completely invisible?" Cedric asks, trying to keep a straight face.

The room became silent to hear the response to the question. Liam feels everyone's eyes looking at him for an answer, but instead he avoids the awkwardness and changes the subject. "Ahhh, you have a James Bond accent, love those movies." Cedric tries to ask the question again, but the rookie quickly interrupts him to ask the doctor a question, "So, when should I expect a fully functional suit?"

"Well, this prototype was better than I was expecting it to be so pretty soon! I just have to change some of the wirings, and you should be doing missions in it in no time," Franklin reassures.

"Well then, we will leave you to it so Cedric and I can take the *invisible-guy* here and show him around," Lyra says, tapping both boys on their shoulders, leading them out.

"Oh, great! Let me just put something on!" Liam tells Lyra as he goes to grab some clothes to change into. He grabs a burgundy hoodie and a navy baseball hat along with a pair of no-lens glasses. "Ok, let's go!"

"Wait, why the hat and glasses? Why not the mask?" Cedric asks, confused by the rookie's choice of attire. "People around town are going to be staring at us, wondering what was going on."

"Oh yeah, it's just for show," Liam answers. "It would be weird if you only saw a shirt and pants walking around the place. People would be *really* confused," he explains as if it was common sense.

"Yeah, I get that but... are you wearing driving gloves? We aren't going in a car. Why not wear regular gloves so your fingers can be covered too?" Cedric continues to nag him.

"Hey *mama bear,* you seem like a cool individual and all but you're kinda killing my vibe right now," he expresses to the wolf as he brings his hands close to his face and tilts his glasses down while he stares at him. He taps his hands against Cedric's shoulder. "Fine, I'll wear the mask and my not too sexy gloves!" He changes his clothes wearing a blood orange turtleneck with a navy trench coat over. He grabs a pair of copper goggles and places it over his eyes. As they were walking out the room, Liam grabs a dark gray fedora and pops it onto his head that was covered by a white ski mask. "Happy mama bear?"

"A bit extra but it'll do I suppose," Cedric replies while trying to give the new guy a hard time.

Liam wraps his arm around Cedric and extends the other like he was showing him the future. "You and I are going to be an awesome duo when we get into some action. Every hero needs a Sam." It takes him a second before he realizes that he was referring to the wolf as famous sidekick characters in movies and shows that are all named Sam.

Lyra shakes her head in agony. "Oh no, there's two of you." Cedric tilts his head to the side with a puzzled look on his face. She smirks and starts to walk out. "C'mon guys, we can walk and mock at the same time."

Cedric looks over at the two of them getting into the elevator. "Let's go mama bear. You know you want to," Liam calls out to his new friend. He lifts his goggles over his eyes for a second "wink!"

"A spot on our team is going to open up really soon because I'm going to kill him," Cedric mumbles to himself, playing with ideas of strangling the recruit.

The trio makes it into the elevator and goes up to the main floor. They exit the building and Lyra leads the way into the city. "Welcome to Hexington Falls."

"Also known as the first city," Cedric adds with the knowledge that it was the first town built after their realm was created.

The city has a historic vibe to it. Tall buildings with a gothic design to them, made from bricks and stone. Strewn overhead, connecting from the buildings, are string lights and pumpkin lanterns that help light up the nightlife along with old-fashioned lamp posts on the walkway. Every lamp post has a corn stock tied up against it. Everywhere you look, you can tell that Halloween is very popular with its citizens. The holiday's decor is heavily scattered across the place. Every store has skeletons and straw bales displayed at each entrance along with a small pumpkin and some inflatables. The downtown area, also known as the Haunting Ground, is where all tourists come to because it has all you need for a good time. Bars and restaurants have indoor and rooftop seating along with balconies where people like to hang out to have an amazing city view in the background. With the busy streets and the creative imagination that was put into all the architecture, the feeling felt magical. Also, can't forget the train that goes from city to city can be heard in the distance.

While walking the main road that ran through Hexington Falls named Coven Street, Liam saw that the city has many shops and restaurants. For more of a dining experience, there is Wicked Taste, which is more American grilled food. If you wanted something sweet, you could go to the Morgue's Ice Cream Shop where they store all of their frozen desserts in cabinets inside of the wall and pull them out as if it was a dead body. The vibe inside is a 50s theme with a twist of a morgue feel. People love to grab an all-black waffle cone with a mystery flavor of black ice cream while there.

The Tricksters Treats Candy Factory next door is where everyone would buy their candy to get ready for their favorite holiday. It has a giant candy corn above the roof that rotates and glows to draw the eyes of civilians passing by. The smell of candy floods out from the factory into the streets which makes it hard to say no to the taste of sugar.

As they make their way towards the entertainment district, they see the Horror Movies Museum that showed appreciation to all popular horror movies from the past to present. From wax figures to props from every film. If you wanted to watch new movies, then they had the classic Hexington Falls Movie Theater next to it. The movie theater is popular for not only the movies they show, but also for their slime popcorn. It is regular butter popcorn, but they also drizzle a green, white chocolate, syrup on top. It can be a little messy, but it was delicious. There is also bowling, arcades, and more places where you can go if you want to have a fun time whether you are with family, friends or your significant other.

The Broom Closet apartment store is where everyone went to shop for clothes. They always keep up with the fashion trends. Everyone has a section there no matter what their body frame looks like. For more fun, dressing up clothing, you have Jack's Costume Shop. His store is always busy. Halloween is more known for dressing up as your favorite character, but Hexington Falls has other festivals throughout the year as well.

The population that occupies the city is a mixture of all kinds of different beings that humans would consider monsters. Most citizens range from vampires, shapeshifters and wizards to goblins, djinn, and ogres. In recent years, some cyclops and mummified beings started to migrate over from other cities within the realm. Each creature looks different from each other, so it is easy to tell the difference between them all.

Vampires, shapeshifters, wizards, and djinns all have the human look to them. The vampires have more of a pale look and a pair of fangs that they can form in their mouths. Djinns have different looks depending on whether they are male or female. The men djinns have more of a steel shade of blue skin. The women have a regular skin tone but have platinum colored hair and glowing green eyes. Goblins have an ashy gray look to them with pointy ears and a sharp pointed nose. Their sizes are normally around three to four feet tall. Ogres on the other hand, are broader and about seven foot tall with a rust color complexion. Mummies were humans from ancient Egypt that were wrapped in linen. The magic that was placed on them was activated by the humans when their tombs were discovered and raided. The cyclops are easily identified by their one eye and being the same size as ogres.

A few blocks in, they walk and explain to Liam about their city and other information he should know about it. He learns that buses and carriages are the only transportation allowed within the city walls. Cars and other vehicles would have to be parked at the Hexington Falls garage near the gate entrance.

As they walk through the nightlife area, they pass a few places where everyone goes to party. The Black Magic was a dance club. Inside, there are a lot of black lights along with green neon lights. Whoever worked the fog machine in that place really took his job seriously because he had a heavy finger with that button. There are other bars and nightclubs they walk past, but they were about to reach their favorite hangout spot.

With bright orange neon lights out front, they set their sights on a bar with loud music blasting from it.

"Banshee's? Like a screaming ghost?" Liam asks.

"Yeah, good name for a karaoke bar huh?" Lyra replies with a smirk.

Bruce, a possessed human-sized warthog animatronic, was outside working as the bouncer. He recognizes Lyra and lets them skip the long line and enter. Liam stares at Bruce because the animatronic had one of his eyeballs hanging out the socket with only one wire still holding on. The bouncer notices the rookie looking at him and gets irritated. It drops the clipboard, and the one working eye turns red.

"Sorry dude," Liam apologizes and hurries inside the club.

An extremely attractive hostess who was human but had a black cat tail and ears, guides them to their favorite spot at the bar. The interior decor had a lot of rock music memorabilia hanging on the walls. Local artists also made paintings of bands like Metallica, Black Sabbath, Korn, Deftones and more that are also displayed throughout the establishment.

On stage is a live band with two goblins playing the drums and keyboard and on base was an Ogre. Walking on the stage was a slightly overweight faun who wore a Vikings helmet over his wild hair and sweat dripping from his forehead. "Good evening, ladies and gents! I am Jon Tulip along with my band, *The Screechers,* and we are going to continue this little karaoke party, but first, I'm going to press pause on the volunteers and do a little number myself!" He wraps the guitar over his torso and adjusts the microphone. The band starts playing an 80's classic from the movie *Fame*.

As they sit on the bar stools, Cedric glances up at the stage and sees the lead singer dramatically getting into the song. "At least this guy's voice is bearable!" he yells, trying to have his voice heard over the crowded room and loud music.

Lyra shakes her head with laughter as she turns to the bartender. "Hey Jimmy, can we get one of your famous poison apples and a rotten cherry slush?" she asks with Liam looking at her, wondering what she was talking about.

"Did you want it as a monster?" the ventriloquist doll asks as he was gathering the ingredients using his telekinesis abilities.

The vampire looks over at the rookie. "Uh, we are kind of on the clock, training the new guy so maybe no monster today."

Liam stares at the bartender wondering if it was real. "So, a dummy is making drinks?"

"He likes the word *doll* a little better and yes, Jimmy is a possessed doll thanks to the heart of mare," Cedric answers.

Jimmy drops the drinks on the counter. The poison apple has a carbonated apple-ginger taste that has a splash of cranberry while the rotten cherry has more of a black slushy drink with a black cherry flavoring in a tall glass that tastes amazing.

"Oh, wow that's delicious!" Liam utters while taking a deep breath then taking another sip, enjoying the bar's signature beverages. "Well, I wasn't expecting to do this tonight" he adds then sips his drink again. Jimmy places a glass in front of Cedric that was called *the witch's brew*. The glass looks like a small bowl on a stem. The color of the drink is purple with edible glitter and dry ice to add a smoke effect. "Ok, wow! you guys know how to make some good drinks!" the rookie yells with amazement, throwing his arms around his new friends. After a minute of enjoying the up-tempo environment, Liam thinks about what Cedric said. "What is the heart of mare?"

"It's a heart that belonged to a creature that was responsible for giving people nightmares. After it was killed, its heart turned to an unbreakable stone and with the help of a dark wizard that slayed it. It became a powerful object that created basically every being you see here," the vampire answers.

The rookie looks over and sees a human-like warthog monster along with some lizard people and other animal-like creatures roaming around the bar. "Sooo, what fears did those guys come from?"

Lyra follows his eyes. "Those came from a mad scientist named Dr. Ernest Monroe, who was obsessed with splicing humans and animals together to create his own creatures. At first, he would inhumanely torture many living things, using body parts at first until he got with another of Dr. Stein's colleagues, Dr. Jekyll. The two of them came up with a serum that they injected into humans which created beings like what you see here."

Liam nods his head. "Alright I didn't see that one coming." He looks over at the creatures again. "What ended up happening to the god wannabes?"

"Well, Dr. Jekyll was caught and frozen until further notice while Dr. Monroe apparently died in a fire while the rangers were trying to get him in custody," Cedric answers.

"Yup, and during the centuries they've been around, every one of them made themselves part of our society," Lyra adds. The vampire takes another sip of her drink and notices that there is something else on his mind as Liam stares at her drinking. "What is it?"

He shrugs it off but sees that she is determined to know what is on his mind, so he gives in. "Aren't vampires supposed to only drink blood?"

She hears his heart pound faster and can tell from his body language that he regrets being so bold to ask those types of questions. Before Lyra had the chance to answer, Cedric interrupts, "She does but vampires can eat normal foods and drinks like everyone else."

"Yeah, we only need blood to keep up our strength. Most of us, like myself, make the blood we drink have flavor because I don't know if you had blood before, but I can't enjoy the taste of pennies. Oh, and we only are able to drink blood in our body's age group." She adds.

"What do you mean?"

"Well, vampires don't age but only if we stick to the

66

blood of the age group that our body is in. If we wanted to look older, we could drink blood of an older age, but we can never drink the blood younger than ourselves because our body will reject it and it could even kill us," she explains further.

The group got quiet for a few moments as Liam processed that information. As he looks up at the T.V. screen that is mounted above the wall, he sees replays of a sport he hadn't seen before. "Ok, so it's good you can't drink babies but now what is all that?"

Cedric looks up, noticing Liam watching the sport on T.V. "That my friend is called *Pumpkin Smash.* It's a popular sport around here. Almost like dodgeball but with magic. You wear an enchanted wristband that, when activated when you run to the middle of the field, you can summon a pumpkin in your hand to throw at the other team. Unlike dodgeball, you can summon a pumpkin any time after the one you throw hits anything."

Lyra adds on, "Right, but the pumpkins don't weigh the same as normal ones do because of the magical programing of the wristbands. It's a fall season sport so the barriers you can take cover behind are a bunch of large crates, blocks of straw and broken-down tractors and stuff like that. Anything *falls-y*"

"Does Hexington Falls have a team?" Liam asked.

The wolf glances at the vampire. "Um, we were the team but this year, because of everything, we just decided not to."

Lyra thinks to herself that this whole time they kept

telling the new guy about themselves and the city but haven't started to get to know him. "So, what's your backstory?"

"Well, my origin story..." he began while Cedric already had his palm against his face thinking that this guy reads too many comic books. "I come from a Puerto Rican background, but it seems like I'm the only one in my family who doesn't know how to speak Spanish. On that note, I decided to move back to New York City where I was born and become a cop like my father was, to follow in his footsteps and at the same time work on my Spanish."

"I can help you work on that," Lyra insists.

"Sounds like a plan," he replies. He continues his story, "My first day in the NYPD, I was just walking the beat with my partner in the Bronx. We walked the same blocks every day, getting to know my environment. Nothing exciting happens on our watch. I mean, we chased this one kid, trying to break into someone's car but he got away. There also was this abandoned building we walked past every day that had a fence surrounding it with tarp on some of the windows but thinking back, that was the only building we never really talked about."

Lyra and Cedric feel something coming up in the story by the way Liam's body was starting to change and even though you can't see his face, you still felt some type of pain was creeping through.

"One day, I heard a noise but when I mentioned it to my partner, he told me it was nothing. I couldn't ignore it, so I told him that I was going to grab food, so I gave him the slip and went to the abandoned building by myself." Liam paused from his story then snapped back from his thoughts and continued. He explained that he found a detective tied onto a chair and surrounded by some gang. He couldn't sit back and do nothing, so he jumped into action. He bit more than he could chew because he ended up being trapped until his partner came to his aid.

"I thought he came to save me, but it turned out that he was a dirty cop. The barrels of chemical waste that were scattered around the building were being dumped towards me and they evacuated but not without shooting one that was next to me."

Both Lyra and Cedric's faces shake in disappointment that his own partner did him dirty like that. Liam continues his story, telling them that when he woke up after the explosion, he heard sirens and called for help. Said that firefighters were frightened when they heard a voice but didn't see a body. It alarmed many people around the scene. A group from a nearby city in Purgintor heard about what was happening and searched for what people were calling a *ghost*. They found Liam but realized that he was not a spirit. The team brought him back to their facility. They helped get him back on his feet and informed him that Captain Vansin was looking for a recruit for a hunting squad, so they knew Liam had experience and sent him to Hexington Falls.

The team gets silent again, but when Liam's eyes wander to the stage, he saw the faun that was singing karaoke, grinding on the microphone stand and acting seductively with his song.

"Well, I guess that killed our moment." Liam jokes while changing the subject and tone back to what it was before.

Lyra and Cedric both put their hands on Liam's shoulders and assured him that he could trust them and that he has nothing to worry about anymore. Liam nods his head knowing he can trust his new friends then orders another round of drinks. They talked more, laughing and having a good time when suddenly, they felt a strong rumble. As they look towards the door, they see people panicking and running one direction. The team look at each other and then run to the potential danger.

Chapter 5

Etta climbs the fire escape and rushes to the top of a nearby building. "Ok, just have to find the perfect opportunity," she mumbles to herself waiting for her plan to take form.

Oozing through the thick iron door she left wide open, a substance started to pour out. It looks to be a thick plum color slime just gushing its way into the streets. After its long body gets out of the underground holding cell, the ooze begins to rise. It grew halfway up the building, and its upper part begins to take the shape of a stubby head and two arms. The beast roars with dominance then drags its body over the back half of a non-vacant bus, slowly dissolving the metal vehicle with its gelatinous body.

A few minutes later, people began seeing the monstrous creature and panic broke out. A smirk took form across the witch's face. "They will have their hands full for a while." As the screams grew louder, she began feeling regret. A part of her is having second thoughts about this whole thing. As Etta stands at the edge, she looks towards the wall where the mayor has a mural painted of her late husband. The paint on the wall is faded. Nobody has been keeping up with it and her heart begins to feel heavy. Falling to her knees, a tear drips down her cheek.

"Etta.... Save me," a voice whispers to her that sounds like her late husband.

Jumping to her feet, she looks around. "Mitch!? Is that you?" Again, scanning the rooftop, she is still alone. Etta wipes her eyes as the distant screaming continues. The witch grabs her bag from the floor and wraps it over her shoulder. Glancing back at the faded mural, the fire grows inside of her. "They're lucky this is all I unleashed upon them... For now."

She peaks over the ledge again to watch the monster attack the city. Devouring everything in its path. Familiar voices from the distance appear. Lyra and Cedric are helping the people get to safety along with one more person wearing a white mask and a hat. "There's our heroes," Etta utters as she watches to see how they were going to fix this mess.

******

"What the hell is that thing!?" Liam yells, demanding answers while picking up a woman who stumbled to the ground due to the chaos.

"That's the jelly-man! That thing will eat everything it comes across and only gets larger by doing so!" Cedric tells Liam while studying the new guy, making sure he was up for the challenge.

"Well, tonight is a good night to die!" the rookie replies as he cracks his neck. Seeing the concern on their faces, Liam assures them that he was ready. "Sorry, I just got excited. I'm good though. Let's go Goon Squad!" His fist punches the air as he runs towards the creature.

"It's Nocturnal Squad!" the vampire corrects him but knows that he was not listening.

"Ok, how are we going to stop this thing? Or did we not think of that?" Cedric asks before activating his wristband that helped to harness his werewolf abilities.

Lyra gets on the radio and requests the captain to send some assistance. The doctor joins the channel and informs them that he sent Frankie over to give them some tech that he worked on that would fire electric rounds, like what the rangers use, that would shock the beast. Unlike what the rangers use though, these blasters are not attached to an electrical pack that feeds their ammunition. These prototypes will use electric rounds that the doctor created and with enough damage, it should disrupt the particles and cause the monster to break apart, making the beast weak and go into a more liquid form to be able to contain it.

Frankie gets to the scene and arms the group with the doctor's latest prototype blasters. Lyra orders the team to spread out and attack from different angles. The nocturnal squad fires their weapons at the creature, but nothing seems to affect it.

The gelatin beast uses a piece of its unformed body to strike a nearby food cart next to where Liam is standing. Cedric quickly leaps and tackles the rookie out of the way. As the werewolf gets up from the floor, he is thrown off when he notices something hard on Liam's chest. "Where the hell did you find a bulletproof vest?"

"Daddy never leaves home without it," Liam answers while trying to catch his breath from the whiplash.

******

Backup arrives as rangers make it to the scene to aid Lyra's team. Etta sees an opening that she has been looking for. "Now that they seem a little occupied, I better make my way out of here before it's too late," she says to herself as she slides down the fire escape and dashes through the alleyway. Some rangers march past her as she covers herself with her hood and blends in with the crowd.

Etta reaches the other side of the city, but there are patrols everywhere. She looks up at the large stone wall that surrounds the city and pulls her wooden wand out of her bag. Struggling to use her magic, she eventually gets a stone to pull out. One by one, Etta manages to make more stones slide out, creating a staircase. As she gets to the top, Etta glances back but only sees smoke coming from where the action was taking place. The witch climbs down the other side of the wall and races towards the thick dark forest.

******

"Ok, I think we're just making it angry at this point!" Cedric yells, hoping for a new plan. He looks towards Lyra for new orders but notices her hesitation. The vampire hasn't been out on the field in a high stakes situation since that night Mitchell died. She's second guessing herself.

"Cedric!" a voice calls out from behind. The wolf turns

his head and finds Samara waving him down to come towards her. As he makes his way towards her, she informs him of an idea that may work. "Try freezing it! They have liquid nitrogen tanks at the Hexington Falls hospital. I'll call them to have it ready for you guys so you could use it on this...thing!"

Liam hears the idea and sees a little boy eating an ice cream cone behind the barrier and snatches it from him. "Official police business, I need to confiscate your delicious dessert!" He runs up to the monster and launches the cold desert at it. "I hope you like brain freeze!" To nobody's surprise at all, the creature absorbs it like it did everything else that stood in its way.

Cedric couldn't believe what he had just witnessed but knew it came from a good place. "I love the attitude rook, but the tanks Samara was talking about will be way stronger." He thanks Samara by touching her hand with a smile then runs an idea to his partner. "Lyra, if you and the rook could keep the monster busy, I can get the tanks so we could end this!"

Lyra agrees and orders Liam to distract the gelatin creature as she moves everyone off the street. Liam walks up toward the blob. "Alright sir.... or ma'am," he pauses to think about it, "you're kinda being an inconvenience, making a mess of things so you have the right to remain silent. Anything you say could be used against you..."

"Are you seriously reading him his Miranda Rights?" Lyra interrupts.

"You know what? You're right. I can't even remember the rest of it anyways," he yells. Liam pulls out a flair from a nearby emergency vehicle and ignites it. Waving the flare at the creature, the monster moves in on Liam.

Lyra radios Cedric to see what's taking him so long. Cedric informs them that he is about ready as he loads up the last nitrogen tank onto the city bus.

Lyra watches Cedric coming in hot and quickly pushes Liam out of the way. "Geez! Does anyone just use their voice and say, *get out of the way* anymore?" Liam utters, almost getting whiplash.

"I'll consider that next time," she winks then taps him on the head.

Coming down the road, Cedric puts the bus at full speed. At the back of the vehicle, he has over a dozen tanks of liquid nitrogen tied against the seats. He has a clear path to the creature. As the bus gets closer, he starts shifting his body and looks back and eyes the emergency exit to escape. "Fangs, I hope you have good aim because I need you to shoot these things right when they hit this jelly man!"

Lyra grabs one of the doctor's shock blasters and aims it towards the bus. Cedric begins running out the back and with his wolf strength, smashes the exit door off its hinges. As he slides on the broken metal door, he yells for Lyra to shoot it. Right when the bus smashes against the creature, Lyra takes her shot but misses. The vampire pulls the trigger again, but the prototype blaster is jammed.

Liam came up from behind and took his shot. "Buenos

nachos!" With the electric round, the tanks explode within the monster and the gelatin starts to freeze instantly. A couple of seconds later, it is frozen and stable.

"Nice shot!" the vampire says surprised.

The rookie twirls the blaster in his hand and blows the smoke coming from the barrel as he begins to brag, "I was known as the sharpshooter in my class." He places the weapon in his holster and walks towards the crowd as he embraces their applause.

"Also, did you really say *buenos nachos*? Wow, you weren't kidding about not knowing Spanish," she adds.

The crowd cheers as Lyra helps Cedric up, patting him on the back. The wolf looks back at Samara and nods at her with a smile. She does him the honors by smiling back with a wink. Liam catches up with them with disbelief that they beat the monster. The wolf looks at the new guy. "Bro, did you really say—"

"Yeah, I got my work cut out for me," Lyra interrupts, hinting that she was going to help Liam with another language.

Everyone is relieved that it was all over. There is a mess to clean up, but everyone is safe. Lyra was about to lead her team back to Banshees when they get a radio call from captain, *"Lyra, get your team and meet me at the station! The portal has been breached!"*

Chapter 6

Captain Vansin gets word that the nearby portal located ten minutes beyond the walls has been activated. Some of the rangers that were standing guard, protecting the caves entrance, had gotten called to leave their post to assist the town when the beast attacked. "It was all a ruse," he utters to himself as he looks out the window of his office. "The creature was nothing but a decoy just so we could weaken our defenses at the cave."

Thaddeus hears a knock at the door as Hunter enters. "Excuse me captain, but I have Gabriel here to see you sir."

The captain is shocked to hear that name. Gabriel is the grand wizard. Thaddeus rarely sees him because he usually stays at the wizard's community Sacred Hills. Having him travel this way must mean that he has something very important to discuss. Maybe it has to do with everything that had happened moments ago with the gelatin monster that was let loose onto the city. Or maybe it has to do with the mystery person escaping our realm into the human world.

"Thaddeus my old friend, how have you been?" the wizard greets with his raspy voice, extending his hand out to him as he pulls down his hood from his cream-colored robe. Thaddeus shakes Gabriel's hand and insists he have a seat. "Unfortunately, my visit is urgent, and I need you to gather your best men and women. We are going to need all hands-on deck, Captain. I've already taken the liberty of contacting teams from nearby cities." The vampire's eyes widened for what he feared was accurate. He just can't shake this feeling that there is a bigger game at play.

Thaddeus agreed, "Come, I will have everyone meet us down at the conference room." Captain Vansin grabs his black trench coat and walks behind Gabriel as they leave the office, towards the elevator.

Lyra and her team burst through the door into the precinct, and they all feel the urgency in the building. "Whoa, this looks intense," Cedric blurts out as the others were at loss for words.

Samara walks in behind them. "Lyra, Hunter is trying to call you. Your father wants everyone to meet him and Gabriel in the conference room for a briefing."

Cedric glances at Lyra. "Why is Gabriel here?"

"It can't be for what happened with *Jelly man*, right?"

"I guess we are about to find out from your father."

They make their way towards the conference room. As they enter, they are met with a large crowd. The room is packed from wall to wall with some unfamiliar faces. Everyone is talking amongst each other and from them eavesdropping, nobody knows why they were called here.

Lyra looks around the room and starts noticing something. "Hey, those guys look like that team from Hickory Lakes, the Shadow Squad!" Her eyes scan the crowd. "And over there looks like the Specter Squad from Apparition Valley! And the Arachnid Squad from Cadaver's Grove!"

"Looks as if everyone from nearby cities is here. Even people from outside sources like bounty hunters," Cedric adds.

"Well, looks like the Nocturnal Squad has decided to join us after all," a sarcastic voice from behind says.

The team turns around to see the group from Eerie Oaks standing behind them. The first member that they saw was the bigger of the group named Titan Roads. He's a Cyclops that stands seven feet tall wearing a burgundy tactical suit. Standing next to him is an almost creepy but at the same time attractive female Jester named Jessy Puzzles. She has green and black hair and a white and black outfit with many weird designs on it. She also has a black fluffy tutu and is leaning against her bigger than normal sludge-hammer. There also is a mysterious lady behind them that looks like a goth western bandit. Thea Vost has on a black hat with straight long dark hair. Under her double-slit skirt was fish-net stockings along with shin-high boots and a black bandana hanging off her neck. Finally, the man with the sly remark is Jason Eriks. He wears a black military tactical suit and a white mask that only covers the left side of his face where he got brutally burnt during an incident with a vampire years ago.

He is a regular human who spent years hunting the

80

creature that murdered his parents. He grew up in the theater scene with his family, owning an auditorium where they would host operas and other musical shows. Story has it, that there was a serial killer that was killing performers, mostly women, back in the day. The victims were found in burning buildings. People say that the killer would burn the place to hide evidence. The only thing the cops found was that the women had puncture wounds on their neck.

******

Eriks was a child when he was playing hide and seek with the daughter of an opera singer. As he was hiding, he realized everything was quiet. Smoke started to fill the air, so he went to investigate and to his surprise, he witnessed a pale man standing over his parents' bodies. He looked over and saw the opera singer lying on the floor as well. The man looked over at Jason and smiled, revealing two sharp fangs. He disappeared quicker than Jason could process. The building was on fire and the floor was collapsing. The little girl that he was playing with found him and grabbed his arm to drag him out of the room towards the exit. The police were trying to get information from him, but he couldn't believe what he saw. As the years went by, Jason would read the newspapers and see that every few months, the same thing happened over and over. He knew what he saw and studied about it.

When he became of age, he joined the military and was in special ops. Jason ended up with the code name *The Phantom* because when he got assigned missions, he was like a ghost. One day after years of silence, he got news that the killer with the same motives strikes again in London. Eriks knew the killer was not human and nobody knew how to stop him, so he faked his own death during a mission and found himself in London to hunt his parents' killer. When he found him, Jason realized that the man looked the same as he did years ago. He knew he was a vampire. The first attempt, Jason failed to kill the creature. He tried stabbing it in the chest, but the man was too quick for Jason to keep up with. The vampire lit the building on fire and Jason got pushed over by the flames. The creature grabbed his head and burnt half of Eriks face off. The man heard a noise and quickly escaped the scene.

A month later, he once again found the vampire in a local theater and chased him down. He ran a few blocks before he lost track of him. Hearing noises in the back alley, Jason went to investigate. He saw a team of oddly looking individuals known as Shadow Squad, arresting the vampire. There was a girl who was holding a glowing wand who was standing next to pale twins who he figured might be vampires as well. The witch opened a rift from the metal portal device, that he learns is called a *Port-Rift*, and they went through it.

Searching for answers, Eriks got word of someone who could help him in Salem. As he traveled there, Jason met with a woman who had collected scraps of a few self-detonated port-rift that she had put together over the years. She opened the same portal that he witnessed before back in London, and he entered. After days of wandering around the mysterious world, he located where they were holding the vampire and found his way to his cell. The vampire remembered who he was, but before he could get a word out, Jason killed him with an arrow through the heart.

The vampire's body decayed in seconds as it became nothing but ash on the stone cell floor. Moments later, he was caught by the prison guards and taken to Captain Vansin. Gabriel appeared and was impressed with the human's abilities of locating where they all were and his mission of killing a rogue vampire. He saw something in him that made him convince the captain to hire the human and even give him his own team.

******

"Oh boy, here I thought that the only crap that I was going to see was that blob creature but nope, they just had to add the Phantom Squad to the list," Lyra expresses sarcastically.

Eriks smirks. "Yeah, I heard about that little fiasco downtown. A lot of damage you let that thing cause. If they let the real professionals handle it, then there would have been minimal damage," He takes a second to enjoy getting under her skin. "But I guess that's what happens when daddy is in charge and wants to give his little girl a million and one chances," Jason gets closer to the vampire and sees Cedric moving in to get his partners back "and poor Mitch. I told him that if he ran with you, that you guys would just get him killed."

Lyra's eyes change to a fiery brown color as she was about to tear his head off but is held back by both Cedric and Liam. "Don't you dare speak his name!"

Jason notices Cedric's eyes glowing yellow as he straightens his jet-black coat. "Oh please, the only way you can go toe to toe with me is if you weren't so scared controlling your full wolf. But no, you'd rather wear that silly moon bracelet and use a sample of its power."

He shakes his head as the captain walks up to both groups. "Are we finished here!?" He looks at Jason and Lyra with disappointment. "You two are supposed to be leaders, so you better start acting like it!"

"Yes captain, we were just catching up and having a little fun," Eriks explains.

"Well, with all that is happening and the danger that may happen, I would say there is no time for any *fun*! Do I make myself clear?"

"Yes captain," they mumble while understanding that there is a situation happening.

"Now, get ready for briefing," Thaddeus demands as he walks away towards the front of the room.

Jason stares at Lyra as she does the same to him. "Phantom Squad... Phan out!" His team all start walking away as he gives Lyra an obnoxious wink.

"Phantom Squad, Phan out? Holy crap that was awesome! Hey, do we have a little catch phrase like that? Man, my heart is racing right now!" Liam blurts out while being oddly excited. Cedric and Lyra both give him a look and then start walking towards the captain, shaking their heads.

As Thaddeus made his way to the front of the room, everyone began moving in to hear what he had to say. Lyra and her team are off to the side. The backdoor opens as Gabriel walks in with a dozen sentinels following behind. With their hoods from their brown scarves wrapped around their shoulders and over their heads, the sentinels march towards the front of the room. The olive-colored armor and helmets on their heads make them look extra menacing. You can't see their eyes through the dark visors, but they have eyes on everyone in the room. The crowd began to chatter while making a path for the grand wizard. As Gabriel gets near the captain, he puts himself behind the vampire, waiting for the captain to begin.

"Whoa, that guy moves pretty quick for his age. Also, who are the post-apocalyptic power rangers with him?" Liam comments.

"That's the grand wizard, Gabriel," Lyra whispers back at him.

"And those *power rangers* with him are called sentinels. They are wizard guards who took an oath of silence to serve in their military," Cedric adds.

The vampire looks over to Cedric. "I don't know why he needs that many guards with him. I guess being 200 years old makes you extra paranoid."

"200!? Holy crap!" Liam blurts out in shock. Teams that were standing next to them looked at them as they were talking loudly. The rookie lowers his voice, "Ok, so Vampires live forever, witches and wizards live more than one hundred years..." He takes a moment as his head lowers with a horrible realization, "and here I am.... Probably going to die when I'm like seventy and with my luck, probably from something dumb like struggling to use the bathroom then BOOM heart attack."

Cedric and Lyra slowly turn their heads and give Liam a disgusted look. Thrown off by where their conversation went, Cedric whispers to the vampire, "Ok, if I didn't already think this before, the new guy has some serious issues."

She can't help but giggle. "We needed a wild card on our team, right?"

Captain Vansin clears his throat, "Welcome, you are probably wondering why we summoned you all here." He looks around the room. "There has been a breakout from our underground holding facilities and as most of you know, the gelatin creature had escaped." The vampire pauses then glances at his daughter and her team. "Luckily, our very own nocturnal squad was at the scene and helped stop the beast from causing havoc on our community." Thaddeus looks down at the podium and then across the room at everyone's faces. "We got a call during the attack that the cave in Mt. Hollow had been breached and the portal to the human realm had been activated."

Whispers around the room begin to wave across from one side to the other. Thaddeus raises his voice over the wave of voices, but the collective of voices outdid his. Leaders from other teams began to calm each other down so they could hear the rest.

The captain continues, "Yes, somebody used the blob as a decoy so we would have our guards down and take advantage of the situation. I have Gabriel here to inform us on who and why, so if he can have your undivided attention, please."

The captain moves aside, and Gabriel takes the spotlight of the room. Everyone is quiet again. "This perpetrator is very ill. We had her locked away and under our care for a while to help her, but she only got worse as months went on." He scans the room as everyone waits to find out who was behind the chaos.

As Gabriel continues speaking to the crowd, Lyra can't help but glance back at the doors as they once again open. Her heart drops as she sees who walked in the room. Mason slowly steps into the conference room, not trying to draw attention from others who are focusing on what the grand wizard has to say. Lyra's eyes give her no choice but to stare at the wizard due to the chemistry they share. Mason has the olive jacket that his brother asked her to give to him the night he passed. As he shifts his body to move around someone, she notices stitching on the back of the jacket where the horseman's sword penetrated. Under, Mason is wearing a white t-shirt along with black pants and boots. Her eyes follow him as he makes his way through the crowd, trying to get himself to an ideal position for the meeting. The closer he gets, the more she sees his doughy brown eyes that make butterflies flutter in her stomach. She feels like everything around her has stopped and he is the only one moving. The memory of his scent fills her nose. Known for a vampire's cold touch, she feels the temperature of her skin starting to rise. As his eyes wander the room, they end up locking in with one another. She quickly looks back towards Gabriel as she did not want to have Mason catch her looking at him.

As Lyra brings back her attention to the meeting, she hears Gabriel starting to wrap up. "This unstable criminal is known as Etta Bettings!" The whole room gasps as Etta was well known throughout the community because of what had happened to her husband Mitchell almost a year ago. Muttering amongst the crowd got louder. "She has become a major threat to us all for she had stolen the very object that had created us. The heart of mare!"

Constant talking within all the other squadrons continues as Captain Vansin walks forward to silence the crowd, "Quiet! We are going to assign all of you to areas of the human realm that she could have gone to. We need you all to be on point with this mission and as quick as possible. Meet with the lieutenants in the back and they will assign you a destination to possible locations where the suspect could be."

Cedric and Lyra's eyes connect, not believing that Etta would be the cause of everything that happened. Liam asks who Etta was and Lyra glances up towards where Mason is and sees him looking down with disbelief. His hand covers his mouth and as she was thinking about going up to him, her dad interrupts, "Are you alright?"

Lyra looks up at her father. "What happened to her? I thought she was going to be fine. They stopped us from visiting her because she was starting a program that would have her back on her feet."

Before he could answer her, Gabriel interrupts, "She had a major setback and became harmful to not just others, but to herself as well." The wizard reaches his hand out and places it on Thaddeus' arm. "I would like all of you to meet me in your office." He walks out the room with sentinels following behind.

Thaddeus nods towards his daughter and her team, "Don't take long." Lyra replies with a nod as well and the captain heads to his office.

"Hey, is that Mason?" Cedric asks, trying to get a better look, but there are too many people walking between them.

"Nope!" she quickly answers. "Let's get to my dad's office so we can figure out what the hell is going on." She rushes while trying to avoid the wizard for the moment.

Everyone proceeds to the captain's office and sees Gabriel speaking to Thaddeus and Danny who was holding a bag of ice against the back of his head. Cedric follows both Lyra and Liam to the captain's desk. Looking around at his enormous office and giant window with an amazing view of the city, he leans over to the vampire. "Oh yeah, I can definitely see you running this joint. Oh, and there is a nice corner where your bed would fit so you won't sleep in when you gotta be at work. Wait, never mind, you'll still be late." She punches him on the shoulder. "Ouch! I was joking, relax!" They try to be discreet so they wouldn't interrupt the captain's conversation but failed.

Thaddeus turns his attention to the team. "So, we have received intel of a possible location where Etta may have gone. It's not one hundred percent but it's something."

"You three are being assigned to New Orleans," Gabriel adds. "Etta, these past few months, was becoming obsessed with the idea of a different kind of witchcraft." He turns towards the captain's desk and sits on his chair. "Some of our members saw Etta researching voodoo and witches who practice that kind of magic."

Liam raises his hand. Thrown off by the gesture, the wizard allows him to speak. "Uh, yeah pardon me my lord or Sir Gabe," he rambles while bowing to him, not knowing the proper way to greet the higher ups in this world. "So, this heart of mare that I've recently heard about, she's going to use it to make more witches?"

"She's going to use it to make the magic of voodoo real, at least, that's the first step," a voice from behind explains.

Everyone turns around to see who is speaking and sees Mason walking into the office. "Ah, yes just in time," Gabriel says, greeting the boy. "I have assigned Mason here to join your team as you go after Etta. Somebody who knows magic could be a reliable asset in a case like this."

Lyra's heart skips a beat when she sees him again. They both lock eyes and as he smirks at her, she feels herself trying to catch her breath. She questions how this man can make her feel weak in the knees and at the same time angry for up and leaving without any type of communication on where he was going. Multiple feelings flood her thoughts at the same time.

Thaddeus voices his concern, "With all respect Gabriel, but they already have Mr. Lin to assist on the magic part of the mission. Also, given Mason's... interesting past with our community as well as every community, I don't feel as if this would look good having him join us. He would be more of a liability with his lack of *magic abilities*."

Gabriel stands up from the captain chair. "Well, I don't have to remind you of how dangerous Etta could be, do I? We need people who know her and familiar faces to calm the situation. The people will understand. Also, Danny may be better with magic and is more skilled with hand-to-hand combat, but he apparently dropped the ball when he crossed paths with her." The grand wizard glares at the young wizard for his failure, making Danny more embarrassed than he already was. He just stands off to the side in his maroon-colored hoodie.

The captain is still unsure of the idea and Mason saw it. "Captain if I may, I know when I was younger, I got into some trouble with the law."

"Money laundering, identity theft, assault, kidnapping and robberies, smuggling illegal substances, please continue Mr. Bettings," the captain quickly interrupts.

"See, I like to think of myself not as a criminal, but as a slight inconvenience. If anything, you could say that I made your men better at their job by keeping them on their toes," he jokes.

"Oh? How would you explain the mayor's diamond necklace that his mother passed down to him?" Thaddeus asks, trying to show everyone that this is a bad idea.

Mason tries to plea his case, "I actually stole it from that pirate gang and brought it back."

"Yeah, but not before you stole it and made a profit from selling it to Death Sail's first."

The wizard saw that he wasn't getting through the

captain. He looks over to Lyra and takes a deep breath as he tries to change his approach with the captain. Mason's voice becomes calm. "Look, ever since Mitch died, I took time for myself to think about what kind of person that I wanted to become. That my brother would be proud of. I just want to do right by him and by Etta. I've also been getting help with my magic these past few months. Also, I have a mean right hook!" He turns towards Gabriel, giving him a wink for his comment about how Danny was a better fighter than him.

Thaddeus examines the wizard closely. "Very well, but if Lyra sees anything she doesn't like, you will be off the case." Mason agrees as he breaks eye contact to look at Lyra. The captain ends the meeting, and they all leave the room.

Lyra walks out as fast as she can, trying to avoid the wizard. "Hey Lyra, wait up!" Mason tries to catch up to her, but she does not respond as she keeps walking away. Cedric greets Mason with excitement and introduces him to Liam. When he looks back up, Lyra is gone.

Walking out the elevator, Lyra begins pacing back and forth in the lobby. "Is everything ok?" The vampire looks over to see Samara talking to her. "Sorry, I don't mean to bother you, but it looked as if you could talk with someone."

"No, yeah it's just the whole thing with Mason coming back," she explains to Samara.

Mason walks out the elevator, "Hey Lyra can I talk to you for a second?"

She glares at him. "No, you can't disappear for almost a year and just walk back here like if nothing happened!"

"Yeah, like nothing happened!" Samara adds with an attitude.

"You think I wouldn't be upset with you? Oh, look I'm Mason and all I got to do is smile and blink my eyes and everything will be ok," she imitates him, trying to mock the wizard.

"Yeah, I'm a pretty boy, look at my long eyelashes and fabulous hair," Samara adds, but this time she speaks in a deep voice. She realizes Lyra is staring back at her with a confused look on her face. "I'm just going to get back to these files...but I got you girl if you need me." She gives Mason a dirty look then slowly sits back down at her desk.

Lyra takes a deep breath, "Look, there's a lot going on right now and the last thing we need is something that would distract us from finding and helping Etta, ok?" Mason nods his head and agrees.

Cedric and Liam walk out of the elevator and notice the awkward moment. "Everything ok?" the wolf asks.

"Yeah, you're late," Lyra informs the boys as she storms out of the building.

"Where is she going?" Liam asks, trading looks with Mason and Cedric.

"Well, from being her partner this long, I'd say that we

are heading to do some research before jumping into unknown territories," Cedric tells the rookie. The wolf pats Mason on the back and follows the vampire outside. Mason follows them as he sees Samara mouthing to him, "*I'm watching you.*"

******

Entering the underground prison, Thaddeus investigates the cell where the blob was being held. "Well, with everything down here, I'm glad that this thing was the only one released."

The goblin mayor, Harold, agrees, "Yeah, nothing too dangerous, or at least less dangerous, with the equipment we now have. The citizens are going to want to know what's happening. What should I tell them?"

Captain Vansin rolls his eyes. "Tell them we had a breach, but everything is handled."

The mayor says concerned, "If word gets out that a dangerous witch is threatening our community then panic will take to the streets captain. Halloween is the biggest holiday in our city so make sure this gets taken care of quickly and quietly."

Thaddeus nods and reassures the mayor that there will be no need to worry, and that tomorrow's events will proceed as planned.

Hunter walks out of the cell and makes his way towards another right across. "The Wanderer," he mumbles as he reads the name that is by the door.

The captain notices the ranger staring into the cell. "You

won't be able to see him. He's a spirit that Gabriel captured long ago." He walks next to Mr. Jackson and peers through the thick glass window. "We know nothing about him so we can't figure out how to release him to the other side and can't let him out because the grand wizard sensed how strong it is."

"You guys think it could be dangerous?" Hunter asks, curious about the spirit.

Thaddeus shrugs his shoulders. "With knowledge of unrested spirits, if they walk the earth for a long time, their minds start to fade. They forget who they are, and they become empty inside. As time goes on, they eventually become restless and frustrated until they completely lose their humanity and become threats within their haunting grounds."

The young vampire stares into the cell for a bit longer. "Have you ever seen it?"

Thaddeus nods his head, "Once."

"And?"

The captain stays silent as he plays back the memory of the moment. He felt darkness but also something very familiar about the unknown spirit. "Nothing, just a ghost," he replies. He taps Mr. Jackson on the back, "Let's head over to the cave and hopefully get this done before the Halloween festivities begin."

Both vampires climb out of the prison where they are met with more rangers. A black SUV is parked waiting for them to arrive. A crowd of people begins forming and the press are taking pictures and asking questions. The mayor keeps the press at bay as he takes it upon himself to answer questions as he let Thaddeus continue with his work. They enter the SUV and drives away.

Chapter 7

Dusting off a few old books from a plastic crate, the librarian makes sure each book is up to standard. When they are ready, she places them on her desk and stamps them with an enchanted ink that gives the book a mind of its own. The book then levitates towards its section and onto the shelf where it will wait until somebody comes to check them out. She hears the doors open and close upstairs. Zoning in on the sound, she begins to hear voices. One of which she is familiar with. "Ms. Vansin, it's been a while since you walked in here."

"Hello Mrs. Willows. Yeah, it's been a while," Lyra replies.

"Maybe a little too long if you forgot that I told you to just call me Abigail," the librarian reminds her. "Speaking of a little too long, Mason, I was wondering when you will be around again. We're all glad to have you back." When Mason opens his mouth to explain, Abigail places her hand on his shoulder. "You have nothing to explain to me. I understand losing someone close. Someone who was always there and just like that, they are gone." She breaks her eye contact with the wizard to reminisce for a moment and then looks back at Mason. The wizard nods his head and releases a sincere smile.

"Well, since I'm here, I might as well drop these off," Cedric says, bringing back books he borrowed a few weeks ago.

Looking at the titles of the books, Abigail read *Family Curses* and the other is marked *History of the Werewolf*. She glances back at him "Cedric, do we need to have another chat about accepting who you are?"

"Wait, so you're a wolfman? Remind me not to invite you over after getting rained on." the rookie says jokingly.

Mrs. Willows looks over at him and extends her hand. "Hello, I haven't seen you around here."

"Well, hola, the name is Liam, I'm the new guy in these parts," he introduces himself. Admiring Abigail from head to toe through his tinted goggles, he changes his voice to a smoother flirty tone. "I'm also very single, wink." He hears Cedric mumbling to Lyra about him saying the word *wink* but doesn't pay them any mind. He drools over her black lipstick that she has on. His eyes wander from her black and white striped blouse, down to her black skirt that matches her fedora.

Abigail puts on her oval framed spectacles and then takes a step closer towards the invisible man. She slowly lifts her hands to Liam's face, taking off his goggles and whispering seductively, "Would you like to know what this little old librarian likes to do for fun?"

Liam excitedly nods his head up and down. His heart is racing, and his mind betrays him when he tries to think of the word *yes*. He doesn't care that there are other people around. Liam is lost in her dark brown eyes.

Abigail lifts the rookie's mask off his head and looks at him. A moment goes by as she looks at his face as if it was visible. A light magenta glare crosses both lenses of her glasses and that's when Mrs. Willows leans even closer. Her lips graze his ear as she whispers with her voice slowly getting deeper, "How about you look into my eyes now."

Her changed voice sounds familiar to him. Liam moves his head back to look into her eyes and all he sees is himself. Rattled about seeing his normal form standing right in front of him, he freaks out, "Holy crap!"

His new teammates can't help but burst out in laughter. "Yeah, so Mrs. Willows is a shapeshifter," Mason informs.

"Oh man, is that what you really look like man? Looks like the universe did you a favor giving your new power," Cedric teases.

"Wait, how do you know what I really look like?" he asks, trying not to freak out too much.

"My husband made these for himself. They see everything. Even what the naked eye cannot," she explains. Her skin begins changing back to her original form as she winks at Liam with a smirk.

Lyra can't help but smile at the situation but then tries to get everyone back to business. "Abigail, we got a mission in the human world and need everything you got on the city of New

Orleans along with its urban legends and books about Voodoo."

The librarian walks to the front desk and opens the wooden drawer. Pulling out a bookmark, she orders it to show Lyra's team what they need to know for their mission. The bookmark begins to glimmer. Floating gently in the air, it glides through the building. They walk past giant wooden bookshelves that reach towards the ceiling. Their footsteps are heard against the black marble floor as the group follows it down to the basement where all the books and info about the human world are located. The sections are organized alphabetically by continents. Each of the aisles are then sorted by countries which leads to the shelves arranged by cities. The bookmark swings to North America, down to Louisiana, and then hovers around books about New Orleans. Mason and Cedric collect the books while the bookmark guides Liam, Lyra, and Mrs. Willows back upstairs towards the magic section.

Moving through the aisles, Liam's eyes wander above. As he was admiring the architecture of what seemed to be a painting of the history of Hexington Falls across the ceiling, he noticed many books floating around and placing themselves where they belong.

"Do you do magic?" Liam asks.

"No, I do not." Her answer was short. She looks around at how alive her library is and then adds, "My husband was a wizard."

Liam caught the word she used. "*Was* a wizard?"

Her hand slides up her chest to her gold necklace she wears with her wedding ring hanging from it. "Yes, my husband and I loved stories and always read to each other, so he surprised me by building me this library. He used his magic to carve spells along the sides of the ceiling and walls to really make this place come alive." She grabs Liam's hand and has him follow her to one of the aisles that read *Mythical Beasts.* "Listen closely to the books."

Liam leans towards the shelf to listen as noises were coming from each book. You can hear the roars from books that are about dragons and the sound of the ocean with thunder crashing with books about the kraken. He is amazed with it all, stunned by how beautiful magic is with a good imagination.

"Liam, help me carry these over to the table," Lyra calls out. The rookie grabs several books about voodoo magic and heads over to the table where Mason and Cedric are. The two were already skimming through pages and taking notes.

"Wow, this city really loves the supernatural," Cedric announces to the group as he continues reading.

"Oh yeah, with that and Halloween tomorrow night, we should blend in perfectly with the locals," Mason adds.

"Hey, I think I grabbed the wrong book because this one is about weird street names," Liam announces.

The others ignore him and continue reading. Abigail breaks the silence from his remark, "Well, I was there for Mardi Gras one year and the seafood I had was to die for."

Cedric's mouth begins to water just thinking about it. "Alright, we can't leave without some Louisiana deliciousness."

Lyra shakes her head at the discussion the guys were having. "Hey, we need to focus on the mission. There's no time for any distractions, ok?"

The boys trade looks with one another. Then Mason throws out an idea, "Maybe something they have we could eat on the go?"

"Quick and easy huh? Brilliant!" Cedric compliments the wizard.

"Hey, there's a street name in Boca Raton, Florida called Butts Road. Ha! Butts!" Liam laughs as he is still on the topic of the book he is looking through.

Abigail leans over to the vampire, "Maybe after all this is over, you should look into adding another woman to the team." The girls trade smiles then continue their research.

Mrs. Willows and the team discuss different things about the city and the witches that inhabit the town. In the middle of the conversation, Captain Vansin walks through the doors along with a few rangers entering behind him. "Lyra, it's time to start going." He stops as soon as he sees Abigail. "Oh, excuse me Mrs. Willows. I didn't see you there." You can tell Thaddeus is caught off guard by the Shape-Shifter's presence because of how quickly his body language changes.

"Good evening, captain. Always a pleasure," she replies as she quickly stands up from her chair. Her face blushes when she sees him in his uniform.

"Oh, believe me when I say, that the pleasure is all mine," he responds.

An awkward silence fills the air as everyone in the room observes the looks between the two of them. "Ok wow, would you guys need us to step out for a moment or what?" Lyra breaks the silence while smirking at her father.

Mrs. Willows turns, trying to hide her smile as she was embarrassed while the captain snaps out of his moment. "Dr. Stein and the others are meeting us at the cave as we speak. He would like to equip everyone with some updated gear he has for you."

They start gathering their things and begin walking towards the exit. Lyra notices Mason's bag slightly moving. He sees that she's examining it from a distance, so he quickly grabs it and acts like it was nothing. The wizard avoids eye contact with her and follows the group outside. She studies him for a moment and then follows the rest.

Mrs. Willows catches up with the captain as he is about to enter his vehicle. "Excuse me captain!" Thaddeus looks over and gives her his full attention. "I was wondering if I could maybe join you since I have read many books about this voodoo stuff. I'm confident if any unforeseen situation should arise, I would have the knowledge to possibly help." The captain nods his head and then gestures for her to ride along with him in his car.

In the van heading to Mt. Hollows, Lyra glances at Mason's bag that he is holding on his lap. He is still avoiding looking at her and she can't take it anymore.

"So, what's up with the bag?"

Mason looks over at her pretending that he doesn't know what she's asking, "What do you mean?"

"Your bag. I saw it move back in the library," the vampire interrogates.

He looks down at it and examines it lightly. "I don't know, maybe my chair was holding it up until we started to pack up." She slowly nods her head with her face expression giving the impression that she doesn't believe his answer.

Everyone in the vehicle is silent except for the captain who's on the phone with someone. Lyra can hear that Hunter is on the line with him. It sounds like all the other teams have arrived at the location and are setting up to begin heading through the portal.

"So, who is this Etta and what does she want?" Liam asks, trying to break the silence of the vehicle.

"Etta was my little brother's wife," Mason answers. "She's all I have left of my family, now that my brother's gone along with my parents," he adds.

Lyra looks over at him as he talks. She thinks to herself that maybe that is the reason he left. That he didn't consider her and Cedric as family. Their relationship in the past was always a crazy game of cops and robbers, but for the past couple of years, it seemed as if Mitch had finally gotten through to him. He was around more and her interaction with the wizard was not about arresting him for once. Maybe that's why it was so easy for him to leave and not look back. Maybe in his mind, the excitement died when he went on the straight and narrow.

"I owe it to my brother to keep Etta safe and to make sure that she's ok, which so far...I failed," he continues while still avoiding eye contact with Lyra.

As Mason looks down at his pants, he slides his hands in the extra pocket of the cargo and pulls out a photo of him and Mitchell. With the thought that he failed his sister-in-law, Cedric nudges Lyra trying to tell her to say something to him. She looks at Mason and is about to place her hands on his shoulder to comfort him, but she stops. Lyra looks down, takes a deep breath and says, "We all failed them both." Everyone looks up at her as she speaks. Her eyes locked with Mason's. "Our job is to stop Etta from what she's trying to do and then help her. We are here because none of us were there for her."

"The grand wizard stopped us from visiting because she was starting a program that would help her though it all," Cedric adds.

"And we thought that was a good idea? She didn't need to be separated from the people who loved her after something tragic," the vampire argues.

"She needs us more than ever and we need each other as well," Cedric says. "Now that the team is back together, along with a few additions, we can all fix this mistake that we created, together."

The captain announces their arrival at Mt. Hollow. Looking out the window, Liam witnesses how huge the mountain is and notices a glowing orange light coming from inside the cave. A flashing green light appears within which means that the other teams are going through the portal one by one to their selected destinations. As they exit the car, they notice the doctor and Frankie off to the side with tables set up along with what seems to be a bunch of tech for everyone.

Abigail is pleased to see them both. "Excuse me doctor, hope I'm not interrupting anything."

"Good evening Mrs. Willows," he greets her with a smile. "My apologies for taking my time to pick those books I ordered. I have just been too busy with everything."

"Hello, Mrs. Willows. I'm happy to see you. Been so long," Frankie greets while having his robotic arm adjusted by the doctor.

"Seems like we all are too busy with our own lives. Might not be the ideal time but I'm glad we are able to see each other now." she announces.

The captain notices Gabriel speaking with some of the teams that have not gone through the portal yet. He finds Hunter walking up to him.

"What are they doing?" the captain asks.

"Sir, it seems like Gabriel really wants to keep his eyes on things, so he's supplying body cams for each squadron," he explains.

Abigail interrupts, giving the captain a look of distrust. "I think somebody doesn't want something to come out during this mission." Thaddeus agrees and then directs Mr. Jackson to get rid of any other cameras he finds to prevent Lyra's team from having to wear any.

Both Mrs. Willows and Thaddeus casually walk back to the doctor as he's assigning each person their new updated equipment. "Ms. Vansin, I have updated your staff into a more helpful weapon by inserting an electrical tip on each end. Now your opponents will get an added shock every time you whack them with it." The vampire retrack the staff and places it in a holster on her hip.

Dr. Stein reaches into a metal case and pulls something out for the new guy. "And Mr. Santos, I have successfully created devices to place on each article of clothing so when you go invisible, the sensors will be alarmed, and it will mimic your current skin condition so everything will be invisible with no problems. Also, I bet it's a little hard to breathe in that ski mask so I made a white mask that will serve you more comfortably." Frankie hands over a box to the new recruit. "Yes, thank you Frankie, I almost forgot to give you this as well." Liam opens it up and sees two black blasters. "I saw how good you were with your aim so I'm giving you these prototype blasters to help with your mission. The light is glowing blue so that means you will shoot non-lethal rounds. If you press this little button on the side, it will glow red and that means whatever or whoever you shoot, won't be getting back up if you catch my drift."

It's now Cedric's turn, but the doctor doesn't want the captain to see. "Oh and Mr. Osupa, I located a moon stone which has twenty percent more energy than the one you are currently using, so after you switch them, you will be able to use more of the wolf's power and speed without becoming a werewolf completely."

Cedric opens his wrist device and exchanges stones with the doctor. "That's brilliant, thanks. Where did you get it?"

"We stole it from human's museum," Frankie blurts out. The captain gives them a look as the doctor quickly orders Frankie to go help another team before he says anything else.

"Well, well, well, the Not-Turn-Out Squad got some new toys. Hopefully now you can do your job a little better," Erik says as he and his team come out from the other side of the vehicles.

"Wow, you really said that with confidence," Lyra jokes.

"Ha! You're going to need some *phan-TUMS* for that burn to the heart!" Liam adds as he slides his hand out to receive a high five from the vampire. Lyra ignores his hand while Jason and everyone else gives him an odd look. He keeps it there for a second, but then slowly slides it back down and apologizes for helping.

Mason steps forward, "C'mon dude, don't act like you're any better. Do I have to remind you about that whole mess in

Eerie Oaks that your little clown caused? Trying to stop me from robbing the Creaky-Tree Bank, riding on top of a wrecking ball and practically destroying the bank along with half of the neighborhood!" The wizard pauses and thanks Jessy for her mistake that gave him an opening to get away.

Jason glares back at the jester as she was lost in the wizard's dreamy eyes. Jessy notices that she's in trouble and walks away. Jason gives Mason a mean look. "Everyone's least favorite brother comes to the rescue. How pathetic that you guys need a criminal to assist you."

The wizard brushes off his comment with a smirk on his face, "A criminal that only two people had ever caught, and I don't believe you're one of them. How many times have we crossed paths?"

Jason became irritated with his failures rubbed in his face. "Next time you walk off the narrow path, I'll be there to take you down. Mark my words!" He stares at the wizard and then walks towards the cave, but not without giving Mason a hard nudge.

"Well done, Mason. I see a lot of your father in you. Brave and always getting himself into trouble to protect the ones he loves," Mrs. Willows compliments.

Mason and Lyra exchange glances with the *L* word being thrown around. He gives her a light smile, but she looks away, trying not to let him see her blushing. The team grabs their equipment as they are called up to the portal.

Cedric notices that Mason didn't receive anything from the doctor. "So, nothing for you? Maybe a robe?"

He glares at the wolf, "Why would I wear a robe?" The wizard points at what Liam is wearing. "Everyone is already going to be looking at us."

Cedric tries to encourage him, "It's the night before Halloween. In New Orleans! Everyone is going to be looking at you if you're not wearing a costume."

Mason analyzes what the wolf is wearing. "Well, hold on a second! What is the difference with what you're wearing? Everything black with a brown jacket with sheep fur on your collar? Wow, you got that at Jack's costume shop huh?"

They go back and forth bickering with each other about what they are wearing until Abigail decides to step in, "Ok children! Get your asses to that cave or I will turn into an Ogre and drag you two myself!" The boys stop instantly and then rush to grab their things. They ran towards the cave. The shapeshifter gives Lyra a wink, "What would men do without us women to keep them in check, am I right?" Lyra laughs as she watches them scamper away. "Lyra, the doctor handed me a commlink to give you. You can speak directly to me if you need anything ok?" She gives the vampire the device and attaches it to her belt.

As they approach the cave, Liam remembers the steady orange glow coming from within. As he gets closer, he realizes why. Scanning the walls and ceiling inside, there are Jack-O-Lanterns mounted all over. You can barely see the stone wall behind them. The pumpkins cover everything besides the dirt floor beneath them. It's all breathtaking.

A couple hundred feet in, there is a green floating orb levitating a few inches off the ground. Standing beside the orb are three giant ranger Trolls that seem to be guarding it. Liam couldn't help but stare at their big noses and sharp teeth. He was happy that they were on the same side. Their bushy facial hair made them look a little scrappy, but they seemed professional.

Gabriel greets Lyra and her father, "I hope your team is ready Ms. Vansin." He glances at everyone and looks unimpressed.

Before she has a chance to reply, Abigail quickly steps in, "I very much think her, and her team are ready for this mission Gabriel." Her words are calm, but at the same time hostile. "I mean, being over one hundred, I could understand being forgetful can be common."

The grand wizard looks at the librarian with displeasure. "Thaddeus, I don't believe that having a civilian such as Mrs. Willows around could be professional with a serious situation such as this especially."

"Well, I believe Abigail is capable of assisting us with this task and I have to agree with her that my daughter and her team, with no question, are ready for what has to be done," the captain responds, defending both ladies.

"Of course, captain," Gabriel nods as he turns to walk away. "But..." he stops in his tracks and looks back at the captain, "As old as I am, I suppose I may be the only one who remembers what happened on their last big mission...or am I wrong?"

The backhand comment silences everyone. Anger begins to fill the air. Lyra is done being reminded about her failure. Her eyes begin changing into a fiery brown color. Before she gets to lash out on the wizard, Mason senses Lyra's anger and places his hand on her shoulder. Her eyes slowly change back to her dark brown shade as soon as she looks at him.

Mason walks up to Gabriel and says, "Excuse us sir, but we are all very anxious with everything going on right now with Etta and we're a little on edge. Now before we start going at each other's throats, we should proceed with our mission."

Lyra feels more irritated with Mason's approach. The wizard never shows any respect for higher authority. He doesn't really show respect to anyone. Gabriel looks into Mason's eyes and then quickly glances at everyone else. The wizard nods his head and then continues walking out.

Cedric nudges Lyra to talk to Mason, but she just walks by him. Abigail glances at Thaddeus as he follows his daughter to get the portal ready for departure. Liam just stands there in silence.

The captain instructs the Nocturnal Squad to stand around the orb. "Your objective is to locate Etta and take her into custody. Try not to escalate the issue if possible." He feels Gabriel staring at him from a distance but doesn't acknowledge him. The captain locks eyes with Abigail and then says to Lyra, "I don't need to tell you that she's not the enemy. We all know her and she's hurting. Whatever has happened to her, we need to get to the bottom of it."

Lyra takes a quick glance at Mason and notices something is heavily on his mind. She is wondering if maybe she is being too hard on him. After all, she isn't the only one going through heartache. He lost his brother. Seems like none of us were there for one another and this is what we had become. Etta is not just Mason's family, but hers as well. All of them were in it together and all failed each other. While thinking to herself, she feels eyes on her and she looks up at Cedric. Lyra knows he saw her looking at Mason since his eyebrows are bouncing up and down. As she gives him a dirty look, she feels breathing from her right side. Turning her head, the vampire finds Liam inches from her face, joining in with all the staring that is going on. Her eyes glow a fiery brown color once again.

"Personal space, gotcha," Liam agrees as he nervously moves back to his spot.

Frankie runs in calling for the wizard, "Mason! You forgot your belt!"

He smirks at Cedric as he grabs the belt, "Look at that Ceds, my utility belt for my Gadgic-Master costume."

"You can't dress as yourself for Halloween Mason. Not even your horrible villain alter-ego," the wolf replies.

"Gadgic-Master? Wait, are you Gadgic_Master13?" Liam asks.

Cedric was lost, "What the heck is Gadgic_Master13

supposed to mean?"

Lyra rubs her fingers against her forehead, "Please tell me that you didn't make a gaming account using your made-up name that nobody calls you."

The wizard stands quiet for a second, "I mean, I know a lot of people who calls me the Gadgic-Master."

The group sighs and mocks Mason and his wannabe super villain name. Lyra claps her hands, trying to get everyone back to the task at hand, "Alright everyone, we are about to go in so remember to bend your knees a little because the exit could be a little much." She looks at Mason one more time before they start up the portal. She shakes her head with a smirk on her face. He rolls his eyes at her and buckles his belt.

"Wait, why are we using this portal again? Can't we use one of those portable ones that I saw when I first came to Purgintor?" Liam mumbles to the wolf.

"This rift stayed open from the first time this world was created. We keep this place heavily guarded to protect it because this rift can't be closed. Many have tried but no luck." Cedric explains. "We also keep all the port-rifts here because the portal helps charge them."

"They're also programmed to only work coming back," Abigail adds.

"Ok, sure but when the Shadow Squad took me to this place, I didn't see the port-rift with them anymore. What happens to it after we use them?"

"They self-destruct, leaving scraps behind," Cedric answers.

"Well, if we hire someone to clean up the debris then maybe it wouldn't have been easy for Jason to find us," Lyra mumbles with irritation at the thought of the phantom.

"Speaking of, captain, can we get a port-rift before we go?" Cedric asks.

Mason's wand tattoo on his forearm begins to glow and his energy wand emerges into his hand. He points it at the green orb and announces their destination. The wind starts to pick up and the dust with it. The shape of the orb changes as it looks like it is about to explode. All the lights within the pumpkins that were mounted within the walls got brighter. Liam closes his eyes and grabs both Lyra and Cedric's hands. "Wait, is it too late to go to the bathroo-," and right before he got to finish his sentence, the orb sucks them in and they are between realms for a brief moment before arriving in New Orleans.

Chapter 8

Newspapers begin to scatter around in the air as the wind picks up. A green light starts to flash as Etta lands on her feet. She hears a splash as she enters the realm, one foot landing in a shallow puddle on the cracked road. She sighs at the unfortunate event. The witch scans her surroundings. Jazz music fades in the background. She looks from one side to the other in the alleyway. No sign of any humans witnessing her arrival. A noise from behind a dumpster makes a rattling sound as a glass bottle drops. Before she can take a step to investigate, a black cat scurries across her path towards the building from nearby. The witch feels her heart skip. She isn't scared, but Etta knows with the bracelet dampening her powers, she is vulnerable to any attacks from any supernatural being. One sign of danger, she will have to make a fast decision to attack or flee. She can't afford to hesitate one bit.

"Hello there," a voice greets them from behind. Etta quickly turns while getting ready to use the wooden wand that she has just hanging within her fingertips. Her eyes examine the man as he puts both of his hands in the air. "Sorry ma'am, I didn't mean to startle you."

"I'm not startled. I'm just trying to decide if I should spare your life or not," she threatens, refusing to lower her wand. "So be wise with your next move," she adds, giving him a chance to speak.

The man tries to raise his hands up higher, but he struggles with one arm. "My apologies ma'am, but I really mean no harm. I just heard noises."

The witch analyzes the man to see if he was a threat or not. As she watches the stranger, she notices that he is in ragged clothing. His back has a hump on it and his face is dirty. Not to mention that it seems as if he hasn't shaved in months. "You're just a homeless man, aren't you?" she asks as starts to slowly lower her wand.

"Yes ma'am, I am," he answers while taking a step back to assure her that he means no harm. His eyes study the wand. "Your weapon isn't glowing. Why not?"

"You've seen those before?" she asks, confused about how he knows what her wand is supposed to look like.

"Of course. If you've been around long enough, you see things. Unbelievable things," he replies. "But why doesn't yours glow like the others?" he asks again. The tech on her arm draws in his eyes. "Ah, somebody put that thing on your arm to weaken your abilities huh?"

She looks at the homeless man sideways, impressed by how much this guy knew. "Yeah, I was trying to get help from people I trusted but instead got looked at as a threat to everybody."

"Well, would you like me to help you get that off?"

Etta's eyes open wide. "You know how to get this off?"

"No, not me, but I know somebody who can. I can take you to him if you like."

The witch takes a moment to think about it. Something seems off about the old man, but she couldn't put her finger on it. She knows that she needs the hardware off as soon as possible so this would help her tremendously. Not giving it more thought, she accepts the man's help. "What's your name?"

The homeless man pulls his hood down and extends his hand. "I am Ian... Ian Gore." They shake hands and then he leads her out of the alley.

"So, who are you? How exactly do you know so much?" Etta asks, trying to get more information from Ian.

"I have been around the world and seen different things in my journeys," he answers. "New Orleans isn't new to the supernatural. We have our stories and urban legends," Ian continues. "The city loves it and doesn't ask questions about it because the mysteries drive the city."

After a few minutes of walking, she hears a whisper in her ear, "Madam Olivia Pierre-Louis." She quickly turns around to see who was behind her, but only sees civilians walking by. Confused by the name, she asks Ian if that name rang any bells.

"Of course, it does! She is well known in the state of Louisiana as the head of the voodoo witches," Ian explains.

"Voodoo, do you know about that?" she asks.

"Well, Hollywood would make you think that it's some kind of dark magic with dolls and stuff like that but it's more of a religion," he explains.

"I see."

"Yeah, many tourists believe in it. They come over loving the idea but are secretly terrified," Ian adds as he tries to pique her interest.

"What do you mean?"

Ian grins. "Well, a lot of people who only have the knowledge of the Hollywood version. They believe that voodoo could be used for possession. Taking control of people or having powerful spirits possess them to become more powerful." He continues walking as he looks at the witch from the corner of his eye. "Some even believe that you could bring the dead back to the living."

Etta stands quietly as she goes into her thoughts. If she raises the witches from the past to enter her body and use their power to amplify hers, she would be able to get her answers on what happened to her husband and take down Gabriel and everyone else who did her wrong and abandoned her. *"With the power of the heart of mare and the fear many people have with voodoo, the plan would definitely work!"* she thinks to herself. She takes another moment, *"But, what if this was a mistake?*

What if it goes too far?"

As her thoughts ran back and forth on the matter, Ian sees the conflict in her eyes. "Some with such power would be able to protect their loved ones from any harm. Too bad all it is, is just made-up stories."

With those words, Etta knew what she must do. There are no more second thoughts or anything in her mind. Her decision is made. Anything to bring Mitchell back to her. Her love for him is so strong that she would go to hell and back just for him. A whole year of heartache. A whole year alone with nobody wanting to be around her. She's angry, pissed off, but with all that rage, she knows she can do what needs to be done, no matter the consequences. "How much longer until we meet up with your *friend*?" she asked while looking around at her surroundings making sure that they are not being followed.

"We are here," he informs. "Just in that building over there" he points to a nightclub across the street.

"A club? Really? You better not be toying with me," she threatens.

"I assure you, he's in there. When you enter, go to the end of the bar. He will be sitting alone waiting for you," he directs. "I will wait for you right here when you are done," he adds as he slowly backs away into a dark corner.

Lifting her hood over her head, she walks towards the club. As she enters, loud music is blasting throughout the building. Everyone that is dancing to the music is all in costume.

Purple and green lights surround the room. With Halloween coming in at twelve a.m., the humans are bringing it in with a costume party. The DJ is dressed in a witch doctor costume and behind him, projected on the screen, is old classic black and white monster movies playing. Looking over the rails, she sees a man in a football uniform drinking scotch at the bar all alone just like Ian said. Etta makes her way down the steps and pushes herself through the crowded dance floor. As she was just a few steps away from the gentleman, he turns from his chair and extends his hand to her. She pauses and looks at him. Slowly, she reaches her hand out and the man quickly grabs her wrist and pulls her close to him. Before she could process what was happening, he whispers at the bracelet, and it just falls off her arm. Shocked at what just happened, Etta looks at her forearm and sees her tattoo starting to glow.

"I wouldn't do that if I were you," the mystery man insists, as he finally looks up at her.

"And why not?"

"Look around. You think lighting up your magic wouldn't cause a commotion in this place?" he explains.

Etta looks around and realizes it wouldn't be wise to do any magic with hundreds of witnesses around. "I'm Etta. Ian told me to meet with you," she informs him. "And you are?"

The man turns back around without a word. He grabs his drink and continues drinking it. Etta is thrown off by his behavior but still pulls a seat next to him. "I know who you are, and I know what you want to know," the man says. Even with

121

the loud music, she's still able to hear the man clearly. "Madam Olivia Pierre-Paul."

Shocked to hear that name again, Etta believes that this man could read her thoughts. "Wait, that name. Where can I find her?"

He slips her a piece of paper with a number on it. "She hates when people disturb her this late." The man takes another sip of his drink and then points at her bag where the stone is. "Also, whenever you decide to use that thing, you'll be better off doing it at the cemetery."

Etta is stunned that he knows that she has the stone. Not wanting to waste the man's time by asking too many questions, she takes in all the information and plays it all in her head.

As she begins making her way up from her seat, that man grabs her by the arm. She looks into his eyes, not sure what he was going to do. "There will be people who will try to stop you. If you truly want this, then you will not let them stop you." They both stare into each other's eyes for a moment until he moves and looks behind her. Puzzled, she quickly turns and looks across the room. She sees them. They came to bring her in. The witch gets up and quickly moves towards the emergency exit to escape.

Chapter 9

A bright green flash lights up the darkness behind an old New Orleans building. A gagging sound echoes the empty alley. "Holy hell! I don't know how you guys can get used to that," Liam says while crouching down to the floor throwing up from the short trip.

Taking humor from his pain, Cedric laughs, "Don't worry rook, after a few more trips, it'll be like riding a bike." He pats him on the back then continues walking. "Now shake it off, we got a job to do."

Mason picks up Liam's fedora that fell off his head and extends his hand out to help him up. Lyra gathers her team around her. "Ok guys, now we need to put ourselves in Etta's shoes and figure out where she went."

Everyone takes a moment to think. As they were brainstorming, Mason came up with an idea. "Hey, I might have something in my belt." He pulls out an old pocket watch. "This was my father's. Took it wherever he went. It's an enchanted tracker. Almost like a wolf catching a scent of its prey and locating where it went. Stole it the day he left. The last time I saw both of my parents." The wizard takes a moment in his thoughts but realizes everyone was staring at him. "Anyways, it's old so I gotta smack it a few times to get it working." He walks off to the side to get it started.

"So, he's been stealing stuff since he was a toddler? Definitely *boyfriend* material," Cedric whispers to the vampire, teasing her feelings for him.

She gives him a light playful jab on his shoulder as she tries to not laugh, "Shut it! He's literally blaming himself on why his mom and dad never came back."

"Yeah mama-bear, not cool. Read the room," Liam joins their conversation.

Mason gets the tracker going and walks back to the group. His eyes catch Lyra staring at a gold chain hanging from where he pulled the watch from. He reaches in and pulls it out. "This was a gift to Etta from my brother. Was an anniversary gift from Mitch that Gabriel had removed for her own safety. I managed to stumble across it along with her belongings when I came back into town. I couldn't leave it there." The wizard puts the watch near Etta's necklace and then clicks a button and a red laser scans the jewelry. It shakes unsteadily, but after a second or two, it becomes steady. The dials swirl around and then stop. The watch floats off Mason's palm and hovers in the air.

"Whoa, that's awesome," Liam whispers under his breath. He looks down at Mason's bag as he sees movement from the corner of his eye. As he narrows in, he sees a smokey blue glow within. *What's this?* As he put his hand inside the bag, Mason tries to grab him, but it was too late. Liam touches the blue light and it bursts out of the bag, knocking them both to the ground. Cedric and Lyra step back to get a good look at what they are dealing with.

"Ok, Mase my man, what do we... Oh, hello there," the figure stops as he sees the new faces looking back at him. "Uh Mase, what's going on here?" he asks as the wizard quickly gets back to his feet.

"You had a ghost in your bag this whole time!?" Lyra yells.

"Ok, I can explain!" He tries to talk but is cut off by the vampire.

"Having a ghost like that is illegal! You know what happens with spirits who don't cross over?" she continues freaking out with his stupidity.

"Look, I know. I didn't mean to!" Mason tries to explain. "During my time away, I was looking for my brother's spirit that was missing during the day of the dead. I was pointed to a cave in Jerusalem where spirits go before they cross over just to see if I see him there. I came out empty handed, or at least, I thought I did," he continues. "I came out with a hitchhiker, and I was going to return him, but I thought maybe I could use him to help find my brother."

Lyra believes in Mason. She knows in her heart that what he did came from a good place. "We have to keep this to ourselves, and we also need to return him right after we get Etta. Ok?" Mason agrees and promises to bring the ghost back where he belongs.

"Awesome! On that note, I'm Ben," the spirit introduces himself to the team with a smile on his face.

"Sorry man, we're not going to name you," Liam informs. "We don't want to get too attached, alright?"

Cedric points out that the watch is on the move. Lyra calls for the team to follow it as she gives Mason a look. The wizard tells Ben to stay close as they proceed with the mission.

"Nocturnal Squad, lights... Out? Wait, that doesn't work," Liam calls out as he's been trying to think of a slogan ever since he heard the phrase the Phantom Squad uses.

Cedric shakes his head, "Bro, you're still on that?"

The rookie shrugs. As he follows everyone, Liam ends up next to Mason. "So, Gadgic-Master. What made you pick that name?"

The wizard looks at the new guy from the corner of his eyes and tries to ignore the question. After about a few seconds, he answers, "I was never good with magic, so I had objects enchanted by some reliable wizards and used those as my magic. Magical Gadgets equals Gadgic-Master.

Lyra bursts out laughing, "Wait, why didn't I put that together? Gadget and Magic? Gadgic!?"

"Probably took you all night to think of that one, did you?" Cedric adds, making fun of the name.

"Hey, it was clever! Better than what y'all would have come up with!" Mason snaps.

Everyone stands silently when they realize that he was getting upset. After a moment, Ben finally catches on. "Oh my god! You merged the two words to make up a name!" They all start to laugh again at the wizard as he gives up trying to defend himself.

They follow the device to a building with loud music coming from it. "Wait, is it telling us that Etta is in here?" Lyra asks.

"Yeah, I believe so," Mason answers, double checking the watch by rescanning the necklace. It still shows them that they are at the right place.

"Well, there you go, all the girl really needed was to party and make bad decisions," the rookie utters. Lyra and Mason give him a dirty look. "I mean, you guys said she's been locked up all this time and you know what these kids say now days *YOLO*! Am I right?" the Invisible man tries to explain his reasoning.

"I don't think anyone uses that word anymore unless they are extremely drunk out of their minds," Cedric tells Liam.

"I mean, I can't really remember my past life, but I feel as if I was kind of a party animal myself," Ben jumps in the conversation and tries to nudge Mason's arm but instead goes right through him.

The vampire rubs her fingers against her forehead, annoyed. "Lord help me. I just need another woman on the team."

The wizard checks out the building. "So, we actually might be good to go. Looks like a costume party is happening so we'll be fine."

"*We'll* be fine?" the vampire questions. Mason doesn't understand what she means. *"We* all look like we are in costumes. *You* on the other hand look, not."

Mason looks at his reflection through a car window. "Don't worry about me, I'll think of something."

Lyra shrugs her shoulders and leads the way towards the nightclub. As they approach the doors, they are met with the bouncer. "Sorry, everyone has to be in costume to enter." Lyra summons her vampire teeth and gives the bouncer a smile showing them off. "Oh, sorry my beautiful vampire." As she walks past security, she gives Mason a wink. One by one the team makes it past the bouncer. Cedric turns his arm device on that helps him show some of his werewolf features. Liam already looks dressed up from head to toe due to his invisibility. Ben hides himself back in Mason's bag when it was their turn up. "And what are you supposed to be, pretty boy?" the bouncer asks with his arms crossed.

The wizard must come up with something quick "I'm the Gadgic-Master, a professional criminal that had a change of heart and now works for the good guys."

"If you are a wizard, then where is your robe? Try again," the man says with a straight face, not believing him.

Mason saw Cedric trying to contain his amusement.

"But I have a utility belt."

"Sorry, no costume, no entry," the bouncer denies.

Lyra's satisfied with the outcome. "Well Mr. criminal, we shall be inside while you rethink that name outside."

Mason became annoyed as Lyra couldn't help herself from laughing. He's still able to hear her condescending laugh coming from the inside over the loud music.

"I guess we are on the lookout then?" Ben mumbles through the bag. The bouncer hears the voice and looks up at Mason. The wizard smiles at him and slowly walks away.

In the nightclub, lights are flashing, and people are dancing. Supermassive Black Hole by Muse is playing throughout the building. The fog machine makes searching slightly difficult. You can't take a step without bumping into somebody because of how crowded the place is.

Lyra gathers everyone for a huddle, but only sees Cedric behind her. She scans the place. "Where's Liam?" Luckily, his white mask makes him easy to spot. Dancing, having a good time with a couple of ladies dressed as sexy police officers, she spots Liam. The vampire marches over and grabs him by the arm. "Hey, I'm sorry to be an inconvenience but we have a job to do!"

"No luck I'm assuming?" a figure appears by her side.

"Mason? How did you get in?" she asks.

"Oh please, I'm a criminal. I've broken into prisons, banks and a lot more fortified place. Also, I'll be damned if you think a man that wears his shirts two sizes too small, could stop me from coming in," he brags.

"Well, this might take a little more time than I expected to find Etta. Let's split up and cover more ground," she insists. They separate and search the place looking for the witch. A few minutes go by, and they are still unsuccessful. Lyra walks to the back of the club and uses her eyes to carefully scan the wave of people. As she looks towards the end of the club, she spots her.

"Over there! At the bar!" She looks closer. "She's not alone. She seems to be talking to someone." Cedric follows her eyes and sees her as well. Liam doesn't know what she looks like, so he follows their lead. "Cedric, take Liam and go around the left and I'll go right with Mason," she instructs. The wolf agrees and takes the new guy with him. Lyra slowly makes her way towards Etta while trying to blend in with the crowd. As she gets to the steps, her eyes connect with the mystery man that Etta has been talking to. Soon after, the witch turns back, and Lyra's cover was blown. Etta gets up and quickly makes her way to the emergency exit. "Damn," she exhales.

The guys come right behind the vampire as she reaches the bar where Etta was sitting. As they were making their way towards the exit, Cedric turns back around to interrogate the gentleman. The man's eyes suddenly gave off an emerald reflection. His body begins shaking for a couple of seconds as his head hits the table. The wolf places his hand on the man's shoulder. "Who are you? What were you talking to that girl about?"

Looking around to see where he was, the man seemed confused. "I-I don't know what you are talking about." He gets up from the bar stool nervously. "I don't even know how I got here!" Cedric looks into the man's eyes and sees that he was scared. Something is wrong here. He looks down at the floor and finds the power dampener that Etta had on her forearm. He picks it up and follows the rest of his team outside. As he makes his way out the back of the club, he finds everybody scattered around looking for where Etta ran off to.

"What happened?" Cedric asks.

"That girl's quick!" Liam yells as he tries to catch his breath. "One moment Lyra was catching up with her, then the next thing I saw was her flying back smacking against that dumpster," he points while explaining what happened.

"She can use her powers again," Lyra informs as she takes out scraps of garbage from her hair.

"I found this by the bar. She must have gotten it off somehow," Cedric pulls out the dampener and gives it to Lyra.

Coming from around the corner, Mason calls out to them, "Hey, we located her! Hurry up!" The team quickly follows Mason as he was being led by his floating tracker down the street. A few blocks down, they see Etta catching her breath. They make their way around her and try to talk to her.

"Etta please, talk to me!" the wizard begs.

Etta is ready to attack anyone who makes the wrong move. "Stay back! Last warning!" Her wand tattoo begins to glow. Igniting it in her hand, the white glow of the wand removing the shadow from her face, she was ready to fight.

"Etta, please just talk to me!" Mason begs. He raises his hands up to show her that he isn't a threat. The witch is too busy looking at everyone that surrounds her. "Etta, look at me!" he calls to her again. Their eyes finally connect. Mason reaches out his hand just a few feet away from her. "Come with me. We'll talk. Just the two of us."

Etta's eyes are starting to get watery as she looks at the wizard. He has the same eyes as his brother, her husband. She lowers her hand and the wand retracts back as the glow from her tattoo fades.

Lyra hears Etta's heart rate slowing down. As she sees Mason calming her down and Etta takes a step towards him. She feels like it's about to be over. Lyra's ears hear a slight noise, a chain falling to the ground. Looking at what it was, the vampire notices that it was Etta's necklace that Mitch gave her when he was alive. She looks back up, catching Etta's eyes as she spots the jewelry and hears her heart pumping louder and louder "Mason!"

"Where did you get that? That's mine!" Etta's voice slowly elevates. Mason tries to explain that he found it, but she isn't hearing anything at this point. "THAT'S MINE!!!" Her voice gets louder as it cracks with emotion.

"Etta please, I can explain! I found this when I came back and was going to give it back to you!"

"LIAR!!!" she yells. Her wand ignites in her hand once again. With a loud scream, she pushes everyone back with a blast. Mason falls back a few feet where he was standing before. Etta walks up to the necklace that is on the floor and picks it up. She examines it in her hand and then places it in her bag.

The witch starts walking away but stops as she hears a whisper in her ear. She turns her head to look back at Mason "Mitchell would be so disappointed." He calls for Etta again, but she ignores him. The witch lifts her wand in the air and casts a spell. A blue light shoots out in multiple directions and over the rooftops. On them are concrete statues of winged creatures. As the light hits each one, they start moving. Eyes glow red as they break free. A loud roar is heard, and the team knows something is about to go down. "Take care of them! I don't want anyone following me!" she demands the gargoyles.

One by one, they swoop down from their rooftops. The nocturnal squad quickly gets back up on their feet and regroups near Mason. "Ok everyone, let's take these guys down and make sure Etta doesn't get away," the vampire orders. The creatures begin overwhelming them as they attack all at once. "Spread out! Separate them and take them out!" she yells.

Mason ignites his wand and begins blasting the creatures. The group tries to break off the flock, but everything is too chaotic. He tries to hold his own, but there are too many of them everywhere he looked.

Lyra glares at Etta as she notices her eyes following the wizard. When the vampire glances back at Mason, she realizes what the witch was really looking at. She turns her head to see Etta ordering one of the gargoyles to do something, and then quickly looks at Mason again. "Mason! The tracker!"

Etta wants the tracker so they wouldn't be able to follow her. Mason can't hear Lyra because he's too busy fighting off the creatures, so she tries to run to him. Before she can take a step, Lyra gets swarmed by the flying beasts.

"Etta, with all respect you suck!" Mason yells, annoyed by what she's doing. From his blind side, a creature glides under him, sweeping his legs up in the air. He lands on his back and hears a clunking sound nearby. As he looks over, he finds that the tracker that was hanging from his jacket, has fallen out. Mason rolls over to grab it but was not fast enough. One of the gargoyles snatches it and jumps back in the air to catch up with Etta. "Hey, asshole, that's mine!"

Smashing her metal staff against one of the gargoyle's head, Lyra makes her way closer to Mason. Realizing the tracker had been stolen, she scrambles to come up with a new plan. She sees her team scattered and facing these things alone.

"Everyone, on me!" Lyra yells. Liam and Cedric rally to their leader, but Mason is still blasting away. "Mason, let's do this as a team!" she yells, but the wizard just cast a spell that helps him take to the air to chase the one that stole his tracker. It was almost like he was running up a set of invisible stairs. Each step he takes, you can see a white glow that disappears when his

134

foot gets off. He keeps repeating the spell every dozen steps he takes.

"I am under the impression that he's not big on being a team player," Liam states the obvious while giving them cover fire. "But much respect on his exit. Reminds me of the Billie Jean music video when the floor shines every time Michael Jackson took a step. I swear, if he ends up jumping on one of these things and riding it in the air, I will die on the spot. I'm just letting you know that now."

"So, what now fangs?" Cedric asks as he lowers his powers through his watch. "Seems like they're all following Mason," he points out.

Lyra takes a moment to think. "Cedric, follow Mason and try to keep the others off him. Liam, take Ben and find us some wheels and meet me on the street." Everyone does as they are told while she radios her father, informing him of the situation.

Minutes go by when, rolling around the corner, Liam and Ben approach the vampire in a city tour bus. "Your chariot awaits my lady."

At a loss for words, the vampire just looks at the big red bus. "Really? We are in the middle of a chase, and you thought stealing this was a good idea?"

"We didn't steal it, the lady was nice and let us borrow it," Ben informs the vampire.

"Uh, I think her freaking out because of seeing a ghost jumping out of the bag may have had something to do with it.

Also, the vehicle was still moving so maybe it wasn't really her letting us use it now thinking back at it," Liam adds.

The two continue rambling on about them stealing and borrowing the bus, but Lyra must keep them focused. "Ok, we don't have time for this so let's deal with what we have and let's go!" She takes the wheel and races down Canal Street to catch up with the rest of the team. Looking above the buildings, she sees Cedric jumping and climbing the rooftops to help Mason. A building or two ahead of him, she catches Mason still chasing the gargoyle that took the tracker. Some of the creatures notice that they are gaining on them, so they break formation and head towards the bus.

"Liam, take the wheel!" Lyra calls out as she quickly makes her way to the top of the tour bus.

Liam follows orders and takes the driver's seat. "Ahh crap," he calmly panics as he places both hands on the wheels and stares at the long road ahead.

"What, what's the matter?" Ben asks nervously.

Liam swallows hard, "I don't know how to drive!"

Fighting off the beast from above, Lyra hears Liam with her heightened hearing and quickly sticks her head below. "What the hell do you mean you don't know how to drive!?"

The rookie studders, "You don't really need to drive in New York. We got buses, taxis and subways!"

The bus smashes against a few cars that are parked on the

side of the road and Ben panics. "Oh my god! We're going to die!" The ghost sees Liam looking at him up and down. Lyra rolls her eyes and then continues fighting off the monsters on the roof. Ben realizes that he was already dead. "Sorry, that was insensitive of me... I mean, you guys are going to die... Not me." He takes a seat behind Liam and tries not to make things any more awkward. His eyes gravitate towards the red and blue lights that begin flashing behind them. "Guys, we got cops!" Lyra hears and adjusts her movements so that the debris from her smashing the gargoyles will fly towards the emergency vehicles to make it harder for the New Orleans police to follow them.

Liam attaches a small Puerto Rican flag around the rear-view mirror. "Marc Anthony, give me strength," he mumbles to himself as he tries to focus on the road.

"We have a very attractive woman fighting what seems like flying monsters on a tour bus!" One of the police officers' radios in.

Cedric sees that they need help, so he makes his way to assist them. He aims towards one of the concrete beasts and jumps while barely missing. Gripping the creature from its feet, the gargoyle struggles flying with the extra weight and is now gliding down. Liam runs over a pothole and the bus starts swerving drastically on the road. Cedric was about to land on the bus with the monster but instead missed and crashes in the windshield on the police vehicle.

"We need back up! I repeat, we need back up! There are people falling from the sky!" Another officer radios for more help.

"Smooth wolf boy!" Lyra mocks Cedric's tactic as the other police cars crash into one another. Cedric quickly gets back on his feet with a smirk on his face and runs to catch up.

Mason is getting tired, but as he gets close enough to the gargoyle, he makes a leap towards it. Landing on top of the creature, the wizard tries to snatch his tracker from its mouth, but the beast wouldn't let go. Struggling to get it, he begins whacking it on the head with his energy wand, making sparks fly from the action. "Get that out your mouth right now!" he demands, like if it was a dog. They both became unbalanced and smashes against a couple of buildings. Mason feels them starting to fall and finds that the creature's head broke off. He tries to quickly cast a spell to help them, but it was too late. They crash on the pavement, but the gargoyle breaks his fall. As he slides on the floor from impact, Mason comes to a complete stop. The wizard rolls off the monster and lays on his back to catch his breath.

"Mason, are you ok buddy?" Cedric calls out as the bus parks nearby. The team jumps out of the vehicle and runs towards the wizard. Mason slowly gets to his knees and a few seconds after, gets to his feet. He stumbles a little bit but catches his balance. Cedric tries to help by grabbing his arm, but Mason insists that he was fine.

"Did you get the watch?" Lyra asks. He reaches into his jacket and pulls it out. Everyone exhales with relief, but the vampire notices something wrong. "Oh no, it's broken." Silence fills the circle and Mason yells in anger, throwing the tracker on the ground. Sirens are heard from a distance as they get closer. Lyra grabs him by the arm. "Hey, get it together. Let's get off the street and figure out another way, ok?" Mason looks into her eyes and agrees. They run down the alleyway and regroup in a dark area where they knew they were safe for the moment.

"Well, we just got our asses handed to us by I don't know what the hell all that was! What are we going to do now!?" Liam questions as everyone looks towards Lyra.

She slowly takes a few steps away to clear her head and then it hits her. "Cedric, you said that you found Etta's dampener back at the nightclub, right? Do you think you would be able to catch her scent from it and track her?" The wolf nods and takes it from her. Cedric powers up his watch and sets it to a low setting. His eyes glow yellow, and he brings the bracelet to his face. It only takes him a couple of seconds before he catches her scent. He looks up at Lyra and smirks as he points to the direction of where she went. "Ok guys, we have to be on guard next time. She's our friend, but she's pissed. We have to work as a team if we are going to take her on. Be smart, communicate with one another and consider her very dangerous." Everyone looks at one another. They know they can't be easy on her anymore. Etta is angry and unreasonable. The best way to help her is to take her down and take her to a safe place.

From the shadows on the rooftops, Etta watches as her old friends plot against her. She knows they are not going to give up that easily. They don't understand her plan. She will have to get rid of them before they ruin everything she's been working so hard for.

"You will have to deal with them first," Ian speaks from behind. Etta looks back at the homeless man and then back at her friends. "I know where you could take them to get them off your tail." She looks back at Ian again for more information. He grins. "It's a bit out of the way, outside the city. You send them on a little detour then give them the slip. You just got to hide our tracks on the way back."

The witch looks back at her friends once more but narrows her gaze on Cedric. This time it's not just a silly little object that she can just break and be done with. She will have to plan something just right to get him alone and off guard.

"I may have just thought of something that could work." She pulls her hood back over her thick hair and then ignites her wand into her palm. Ian grins and then follows.

Chapter 10

Sitting at her station near Mt. Hollow's cave, Abigail hears her radio. It was staticky at first, but seconds later it became much clearer. *"Abigail, it's me, Lyra!"*

The captain quickly races over and hovers behind the librarian. "Hello, Lyra come in," she replies, trying to communicate with the vampire. Lyra informs them that they have located Etta and are in pursuit as they speak.

"Lyra, can you confirm that it's really Etta?" the captain interrupts.

"Yes sir, she tossed us around at first then brought to life a handful of statues to attack my team. She wasn't very happy to see us," she informs her father. Mrs. Willows and Thaddeus both glance at each other while Gabriel pops his head over to listen in.

"She got the dampener off?" the captain asks to get confirmation of the situation. Lyra informs him that she met with some human that helped her and is now on her way out of the city. "Just be careful, alright?" his voice softens. "Let us know if you need any backup."

Abigail's hand slides up the captain's arm. He feels her

eyes on him. He thinks to himself about how Etta is a very talented witch. Mitchell trained her very well. He knew Mason had the same training, but he never dedicated himself to it. Etta is also fueled by anger and pain. She will be on point with everything she does. One mistake by Lyra or her team and someone could get really hurt. Every mission can be extremely dangerous and no matter what, Lyra and her team have always come on top. Thaddeus trained her, pushed her to be the very best warrior she could be. But this time something feels off. His eyes move to the corner, and he finds the grand wizard standing there looking, maybe because Gabriel was mixed in somehow.

"So, Etta is in Louisiana then," the wizard states. Abigail turns around to answer, but is interrupted by Gabriel, "Well Mrs. Willows, call back the other teams. We found our problem."

Angered by the poor choice of words that he used; the shapeshifter opens her mouth to give him a piece of her mind. Thaddeus quickly steps in and agrees with the wizard. She looks up at him wondering why he doesn't want her to say anything back, but by the look of his face, she trusts him. "Of course, I'll reach out to everyone right now."

Gabriel begins walking away but stops. "Oh, and Captain Vansin, I would like eyes on the situation or send another team in because it seems like your daughter's team doesn't have a bodycam on any of them."

Thaddeus disagrees, "That won't be needed. I'm confident that Lyra and her team will do what they need to do. Throwing another team could do more damage to the mission than good."

Gabriel raises an eyebrow, "Well, I hope you know what you are doing captain."

"It's my job to know and the fact that I am the one in charge of this operation, I would appreciate it if you would let us do what we came here to do," Thaddeus replies with a stern tone.

Gabriel nods his head and then leaves. He looks back at the captain as he never takes his eyes off him. He smirks once more and then vanishes. Captain Vansin walks towards the wooden wall and places a map of New Orleans across it. He marks his daughters' last known location and where they are headed. Abigail walks up and helps look to see where Etta might be off to. The radio is silent, and rangers are in and out assisting them.

"Thaddeus, may I ask you a question?" she asks. The captain looks into her brown eyes and nods. "There's something I've been meaning to talk with you about and it's about Gabriel." A concerned look falls over her face and Thaddeus is all ears. "I know you are familiar with the rumors of the notorious cult."

Thaddeus looks away with his hand rubbing against his face. "You think he's part of it?" He glances at Abigail, and she nods. He looks out of the little wooden shed that they are in and closes the door. The vampire pulls out his phone and logs into his photos. "It's been a century since anyone heard of them, but within the past year, I have been finding these markings on walls and other places. For all we know, it could be kids doing dumb things." He shows her several pictures of bathroom walls and other places that were all bearing the same wording, "The Higher

Power" with a black crown on top.

Looking closer at each photo, Abigail notices something different with the newer markings that the old ones did not have. She pulls out a book from her bag and opens it up. Flipping through pages, she finds what she was looking for. "The markings back then only had a plain black crown on them."

Confused, Thaddeus looks at the book carefully, then at the picture he recently took. "Inside the crown has small inscriptions." He looks closer to try to read what the newer marking says. *The First Borns Shall Rise Again.*

Mrs. Willows shrugs her shoulders. "I guess over the years they made a catch phrase but given that they have it written within the crown, I would assume it must mean something more important."

Hearing footsteps closing in on them, the captain quickly puts everything away. Busting through the door is Eriks. "Well, I guess Lyra was given the right hand in all this." His team stands by the door. Jason seems irritated by the outcome but tries to keep his composure. "Feel free to call them off and let a real team swoop in and handle this professionally," he snarks.

Pushing his way between the phantom squad, Hunter enters the room. "My apologies captain but the doctor would like to see you."

Abigail taps Eriks on the shoulder, grinning, "Maybe next time sport." She follows the captain out the door and tells Mr. Jackson to take over at the command center.

Walking outside, they see all the other teams passing through the portal and setting up camp at the site in case any of them are needed. A few yards away, they see Frankie assisting the doctor by moving heavy objects. The doctor seems to be working on a potion alongside Danny Lin.

"Ah, captain Vansin, you're right on time," the doctor greets. "Frankie, when I say so, push the lever all the way up," he calls out. Frankie places the crate he was holding down and walks to the other side where the doctor directed. Forgetting for a moment that Thaddeus is there, he lets Danny take over with a small spell casting. "My apologies captain, but what we are whipping up is a very delicate potion," he explains. "An old idea by an old colleague. With the help of science and some magic, I have come up with a way to have vampires, such as yourself, be able to walk under the human sunlight."

Impressed with the groundbreaking news, Thaddeus and Abigail watch closely as the doctor works. Danny informs Dr. Stein that it was time, and he yells for Frankie to pull the lever. Steam whistles from the machine as the whole table shakes. Danny ceases his powers, and the doctor carefully takes one last ingredient and adds one drop from the bottle into the glass. The jar seems as if it was about to overflow, but then stops at the rim. The Purple foam slowly dissolves, and the potion is ready.

The grand wizard, along with other witches and wizards, gather around. Jason and his team watch from the distance unimpressed. Frankie walks behind the doctor and pats him on the back.

"Well, did it work?" The captain asks anxiously.

The doctor grabs the bottle with his mechanical fingers and raises it into the air to get a good look at it. It continues bubbling a little, but it ends up calming down. He stirs the glass around as if it was a glass of wine. Dr. Stein turns towards Thaddeus, "I'm not as successful with potions as my old colleague was but yes, it seems we are indeed successful."

The crowd applauds at the new breakthrough. The captain shakes the doctor's hand and then looks at Mrs. Willows as they trade smiles. This is the first step of having vampires be able to walk out in the human sun. Gabriel follows Thaddeus and congratulates the doctor as well.

While everyone is busy, Abigail rubs the captain's back. "We need to talk about what we are going to do with what we were discussing about."

The captain agrees and they slip away back to the wooden shed where Hunter has been manning the radios. "For the past few months, I have created a list of names of some potential suspects," he whispers as they make their way through the crowd.

Abigail is surprised and nudges him, "Oh you do? Am I on that list captain?"

Thaddeus stops and turns his body in front of hers. "Your name is on my list but not about being a suspect." He smiles at her and has his lips shift closer to hers.

Breaking up the moment, Abigail slides her finger over

146

his mouth. "Ok, I know you thought that sounded romantic but that came across kinda creepy."

"Oh, shut up, we got to go," he replies as he thinks about what he said. They laugh it off and continue walking. He is silent for a moment to gather his thoughts. "My apologies Mrs. Willows, but it has been a very long time since I tried to be romantic with anyone." Abigail leans her shoulder against his. He takes another moment as he tries to open with her. "The last time I was ever this way with someone it was with Lyra's mother. And before that I was too busy fighting one war after another."

Abigail understands how Thaddeus feels. She too has lost a loved one. It's hard getting back on that horse without being a little rusty. She never tried to love again because she felt like it was betraying the dead. Abigail grabs his hand and holds it tight. "We both got some work to do, but luckily we aren't expecting perfection from one another."

"Excuse me sir, but I accidentally came across this book with this page open about some cult and noticed the similarities with some of the inmates I've put away," Hunter interrupts as he has some information.

The captain looks over to Abigail and then back at the young vampire. "Well, welcome aboard my boy, we have a few things we need to discuss."

Chapter 11

Leaving the city, Mason hotwires a car for them to travel in. "You see rook, when we are in a chase or just need a ride, you have to get something like this."

"An old piece of crap *stranger danger* van?" Liam responds.

Mason gives him a look and then turns his eyes back on the road. "No, this is a low-profile piece of machinery. Sure, it's junk but it helps us get the job done."

"Well, I would definitely leave the description as a *stranger danger* van," Lyra jokes. She catches the wizard glancing at her through the rearview mirror. Her heart skips, then she returns to looking out of the window.

"What's all the way out here that Etta's after?" Cedric asks as he continues following her scent. Mason shrugs at the question.

"You think she's taking us all the way out here just to kill us?" Liam adds to the question. Everyone stood silent at the possibility.

"I mean, if I had powers like that and I had someone chasing me, I probably would definitely lead you guys to your death," Ben chimes in the conversation.

Lyra notices Mason's face. He seems upset. She knows that Mason will never accept the thought of her to be a killer. Etta is his sister-in-law. We all knew her, but she's in a different mindset right now, so anything is possible. "Well, no matter what kind of person she is at this moment, she is still our friend. Nothing has changed," the vampire announces.

"So, trying to kill your friends and still being friends after? Check," Liam mumbles to himself. Cedric and Lyra can't help but hear him with their hearing abilities. They both chuckle to themselves.

The night gets later. The fog is rising. Cedric tells Mason to pull off the road and down a dirt path. Etta led them to a farm miles away from the city. All the lights seem to be turned off and not one person is in sight. They get out of the van and wander the land.

"Let's split up and cover more ground. The sun is going to rise soon so we must hurry," Lyra announces.

Liam disagrees with the idea, "Split up? In real horror movies, when they split up, it gives the killer easy targets to pick them off one by one!"

"In that dog cartoon with those hippy kids, they split up all the time and they all survive," Ben adds.

"Yeah, movie buffs are going with you," Mason informs

the vampire. "I'll take Ced's."

Lyra bites her tongue. "Fine, but Ben goes with you because that's your mess. Also, you guys check out the house and we will look around outside." The wizard agrees and has the ghost hide back in the bag with no talking.

The team splits up and goes their assigned ways. Lyra and Liam roam outdoors scouting the land. First, they check out the shed to see if the witch is hiding out there.

"Nothing here, just tools and a tractor. Etta what are you up to?" she speaks under her breath. They continue towards what seems to be a pumpkin patch. A vampire's eyes can see clearly in darkness, so she scans the field, but still does not see any signs of the witch.

"Oh crap, something is telling me that she's going to be in there," Liam points towards a corn maze. Lyra smiles and makes her way to the maze. "It's a little unsettling that you are enjoying being in creepy places," he says.

Lyra ignores him and continues walking. The rookie drags his feet behind her into the field. He pulls out his blaster from the holster and points a flashlight as he carefully takes steps following the vampire. Lyra seems calm as Liam jumps every time he hears something within the corn.

The radio calls and Lyra answers it, "Hey, did you find something?"

"Yeah, we found the owners of the property. They seemed to be knocked out," Cedric responds. *"Mason just checked each*

one and they all have a pulse. He said it looks like a spell, so Etta must be close by. Be careful," the wolf adds.

The vampire places the radio back at her hip and slowly follows the path through the maze. Liam is a bit more nervous than before as he stays on his guard. The night seems peaceful. It is quiet as the wind blows. Along the dirt path are cut out pictures of cartoon zombies for when the human children roam through. One of the cutouts was broken and the piece of wood that was holding it up from behind is sticking out and catches on Liam's coat. Immediately he starts freaking out and pulls his coat free as he trips over a piece of corn that has been lying on the ground. Lyra turns around to see what was going on and laughs. She reaches out her hand to help him up. As he gets up, the rookie notices something behind her. Something hovering over them with its arms spread open.

"Behind you!" he yells as he grabs her by the arm and tosses her to the side. Liam bends over to pick up his flashlight and points it at the object. Lyra quickly gets up and jumps back into action.

"Really? You pushed me aside to save me from that!?" she says, annoyed.

It takes him a second to realize that it was only a scarecrow that he was freaking out about. He nervously chuckles, "Whoopsie. My bad, that's on me." She walks past him, shaking her head. "I said whoopsie!" he says once more thinking it would make things better. Liam continues following Lyra with his head down. He starts laughing at himself as he looks back at the scarecrow that startled him. As his flashlight points at the scarecrow, he freezes. "Wait, where the hell did he go?"

Lyra glares back at him but then sees that the scarecrow wasn't there anymore. "Did you touch it and it fell?" she asks. The rookie shakes his head. Her hand reaches down to the radio and calls the others, "Hey guys, I think we may have some company in the corn maze." Cedric answers back letting them know that they are on their way.

They begin to hear movement around them. It seems quick. Maybe multiple hostiles. Liam flashes his light in each direction to see if he sees anything. The movement stops. He looks at the vampire and gives her multiple hand gestures. Not knowing what the hell he's trying to say, she guides him aside as she walks through. Hearing a snap, Liam looks to the side and finds a shadowed figure. He slowly raises his light to get a better look but sees nothing. Right before he lowers his flashlight, a pitchfork rips through the cornstalk. Liam jumps back and grabs his weapon to begin shooting. Lyra pulls her staff from her waist and clicks the button to extend it. The threat vanishes, but seconds later it seems to make its way around to attack from the other side. She blocks the attack and swoops her staff into the stalk, but it vanishes once more.

They hear ruffling in the distance. They keep turning to follow the noise. "This thing is fast for something made from hay," Liam mumbles to the vampire.

Lyra runs to the pole where the scarecrow had been

hanging from to see if she could get a better view. "Uh, I don't think we are dealing with only one." She sees three similar poles across the maze that are empty as well. Lyra leaps back down as she hears something moving towards them. "Ok Liam, stay close and move quickly. Let's try to get them to play this our way and fight them in the open," she instructs.

He follows Lyra as they try to retrace their way back to where they came. From left and right, pitchforks scrape through as they dodge their attacks. Some of them Lyra had to block. Liam shoots some taser rounds throughout the field to slow them down.

"Here! I see the exit!" he calls out. Racing, a body leaps out and tackles Lyra to the ground. One of the scarecrows is on top of her with another coming from behind, and the other two are coming from the sides. Liam tries to load another clip into his gun but is having trouble. Lyra yells for him to run and get the others, so he turns and runs. After a few steps, he looks back and knows he can't just leave her. He must suck it up and do his job. Loading up his weapon, he walks back towards Lyra and empties the whole clip into the creature above her. The taser ammo shocks the scarecrow so much the dry straw begins to burn and catches on fire. "Looks as if he had the *hots* for you," he says sarcastically.

Lyra rolls her eyes as she makes her way up to her feet. From the side of him, another scarecrow launches out and grabs Liam by the throat. This one was bigger than the others. "Oh god, you have no business being this strong!" Struggling to breathe, he tries to figure out a way out of the situation.

"Normally I would tell you to buy me a drink first," he jokes while fighting to breathe. The creature snarls at him as it squeezes tighter.

The vampire takes a step forward to help but is cut off by another and remembers the one coming from behind who is wielding two sickle blades. "Liam, kick him!" she yells right before she dodges one attack from behind.

He looks down at the creature and then back into its cutout eyeholes. "You seem like a kinky guy so you can thank me later!" With all his energy, he pulls his leg back and then swings it forward as he kicks the monster between its legs. Realizing the scarecrow didn't react to the strike, Liam decides to try it again. He tries a couple of more times, but nothing seems to affect the monster.

"At this point you're just pissing it off even more!" Lyra shouts as she fights off the other two. She bends down and extends her staff and in one strike, she spins around, swooping the two creatures off their feet and to the ground. Hearing Liam's breathing fading, she throws her weapon, and it stabs through the scarecrow's head. Its hands loosen up and Liam breaks free. Lyra pulls her staff out of the creature's head with the fabric that was covering its face getting caught and pulled off as well.

Making it out of the maze, they see in the distance Mason and Cedric running towards them. Lyra spots Etta standing on top of the farmhouse with her wand in the air. The wind picks up and what looks like lightning flying out of the witch's wand and scattering into the night sky.

Mason looks back and sees Etta. He turns back to Lyra and finds three beings emerging from the corn maze behind her. He runs towards her and ignites his wand.

"Wait! Mason, do you hear that?" Cedric yells.

The wizard stops to listen. The noise sounds like wings. Hundreds, maybe thousands of wings flapping in the air. If possible, the night sky appears to be getting darker by the minute. Mason shoots a beam of light into the air and then sees them. A murmuration of birds heading their way. They stand back-to-back as the crows circle above. A few of them land around objects scattered close by. Mason looks at the one closest to them. He notices that their eyes are pure white. The wizard looks back at Etta and knows that she's controlling them. The crows flying in the sky start making their way around. They seem like they are forming a train of birds as they fly down towards the team.

"They're attacking!" Ben yells as he peeks out of Mason's bag.

The wizard points his wand in the air and casts a spell that shields them from their attacks. The crows smash against the bright white barricade but are unsuccessful in penetrating it. Crows keep crashing into it, wave by wave, but Mason is holding onto the spell as strong as he can.

Lyra and Liam have their hands full with what they are facing. The invisible man investigates his gun. "Whoopsies." The vampire looks over to see what was wrong. "Ok, I may have gotten a little trigger happy back in the maze," he tells her, embarrassed with his hand placed against his face.

"Well, I hope you are good with your hands because we got to work together on this," she informs.

The scarecrows attack at the same time to overwhelm the two heroes. The other three are trying to figure out how to get rid of the birds. Both sides are just holding on playing defense.

"Hey guys, that very attractive witch lady is gone," Ben informs the group.

Cedric looks back and sees that Etta isn't there anymore. "Maybe this was just a distraction?"

Mason agrees as he thinks of a plan. He sees Lyra fighting off these monsters alongside Liam and they seem to have that under control, so he doesn't need to do anything drastic. "Ok Ben, since they can't really hurt you, I need you and Ced to help separate the birds so we can play some offense," he explains. "I'm going to make an opening behind us, and you guys spread out so I can attack," the wizard instructs. He lowers the shield, and they begin running out.

Cedric's eyes get drawn towards the maze as he spots Etta standing at the entrance. She winks at him then walks inside.

"I see her!" the wolf yells. Mason tries to keep Cedric to stick with the plan but is unsuccessful. Cedric thinks if he catches Etta, that everything will stop, and his friends will make it out unharmed. The wolf runs towards the witch, ignoring Mason. He reaches the entrance to the maze and then slows down. The wolf wants to proceed with caution because he knows

Etta is dangerous. As he takes a few steps in, he hears a noise coming from around the corner. He follows the sound, but as he turns the corner to investigate, the only thing he sees is a man on the ground. He hurries over to what seems to be a homeless man that needs help. Cedric places a hand on the man's back and feels that he has a hump. The mystery man picks his head up and grins as his eyes look past the wolf. Cedric follows the man's vision and looks back. In seconds, Etta is behind him, and she casts a spell as she points her wand in his face. Violet sparks shoot out and goes straight to his nose. The wolf covers his face as he collapses on the floor in pain.

"Ok good, now finish him!" Ian orders as he gets up from the floor. Etta glances at him and shakes her head. His face changes as he is upset at the witch's decision. He looks at Cedric's arm and smirks. "Fine. I'll just deal with the hand that's given to us." Ian kneels and turns Cedric's arm device to full power.

"Wait, you can't! He hasn't had enough training in that form! Cedric won't be able to control himself!" Etta panics.

Ian glares at her. "You want your husband back, don't you?" She nods as she looks down. "They won't let you do what needs to be done. They will only try to stop you," he reminds her. Ian knows that she's unsure of what she wants. The fight that was in her before is slowly fading. "You told me yourself that you would do anything to bring your love back to you. unless you are now fine with the fact that he's dead and won't feel that love ever again?" Ian questions.

Etta picks her head back up, but this time the fire in her eyes is back. Her chin is up as she nods at Ian, thanking him for keeping her eyes on the prize. They quickly run off when Cedric starts his transformation into a beast.

Lyra finishes the scarecrows, leaving them as piles of straw on the ground. A loud howling from the maze is heard. She quickly turns her head to investigate. "Cedric?" she calls out, looking for a response but gets nothing. The vampire cautiously moves closer "Cedric, are you ok?" She looks back at Mason as he and Liam are now on the offense fighting off the crows, or at least attempting. Rustling comes from within the maze. "Cedric? Are you ok?" she calls calmly, having an idea of what is happening to her friend.

Silence fills the area for a moment. The sound in the background fades off. The vampire stops in her tracks. She parts her lips and slowly exhales. Jolting from the maze is Cedric who is a full werewolf. He lets out a loud roar and leaps towards Lyra to attack her. She runs and slides under the beast. His razor-sharp claws barely slice her face. They both turn towards each other, and their eyes lock.

Mason hears the roar and sees Lyra and Cedric fighting. The wolf keeps throwing himself at the vampire, but she keeps dodging and blocking the blows. Mason's eyes are struggling to keep up with how fast they are moving. He feels his concentration with his fight is breaking, so he quickly makes another shield around him to block the crows' attacks.

"Mason, I have an idea!" Liam calls out from behind a

truck.

The wizard instructs Ben to cause a distraction so he can slip under the birds' radar and get closer to Liam. The ghost did just that as he ran across the field, flapping his arms around and screaming. Many of the crows take notice and go after him.

Mason reaches the truck where Liam took cover. "Ok, so there was a movie I saw when I was a kid and an evil witch turned into a dragon..."

"Yeah, no you might've seen one too many princess movies because that's not what we do," the wizard interrupts. Liam pauses to think of another idea but comes up with nothing. After a moment, Mason's eyes light up with an idea. "Wait, I may not be able to turn into a giant lizard, but I might be able to create one! I just need some fire."

Liam tries to think of where they could find fire. He looks around to see what they can use. Banging the back of his head against the truck, he gets an idea. "We can blow up the truck!"

Mason looks at him and smiles. "Let's blow this truck up!" Overly excited, they back away from the vehicle and leave the gas tank exposed. Mason aims his wand at it and fires an exploding spell. The blue beam shoots straight into the gas tank and blows it up.

The explosion catches the attention of the crows, and they start heading back towards the guys. The wizard quickly casts another spell to manipulate the fire and shapes it to look like a hydra.

Liam is amazed at what he was witnessing, watching the three-headed beast take form. "This is the happiest day of my life!"

The fiery hydra and the crows charge at one another, but right before they clash, Mason has his creation explode, causing the birds to fly back and try to catch themselves from falling. One lands near Ben, but before he tries to kick it with his ghostly foot, he discovers something. "Hey, I think the spell that the witch did on them is gone now!"

Relieved with his findings, Liam and Mason give each other high fives. The celebration is cut short when they see Cedric grab Lyra by her leg and smash her through the wooden barn.

"Lyra!" Mason yells as he runs towards where they are fighting.

The vampire gets up and dusts herself off. Cedric barges in where the hole is in the wall and growls at her. "Sorry wolf boy, but we gotta end this little dance," she mumbles. Lyra picks up her staff from the floor and leaps over the wolf, hitting him over the head. Cedric roars, getting angrier. He charges at Lyra, but she sees an orange glow swirling around the wolf's body. Mason gets a hold of Cedric for the moment. The beast, filled with rage, tries to escape, but the power is too strong.

"Mason, we have to lower the level on Cedric's armband!" she calls out. Attempting to get near him, Cedric starts clawing at anyone who gets too close.

"Cedric, no! Bad boy!" the wizard yells as one of his claws almost rips off Lyra's face.

Footsteps are heard nearing the wolf, but nobody is seen. "I got this guys," an unseen voice says. Cedric's armband starts making beeping sounds and he slowly starts turning back to his human form. Mason releases him from the spell and Liam appears next to him. "Well, finally my powers came in handy."

"Nice job rook!" Lyra says, while catching her breath.

Cedric regains his human form as he lays on the floor unconscious. Mason grabs a red plaid button down shirt that he saw laying around and places it on Cedric's naked body. They move him to a more comfortable spot until he wakes.

"Wow, that was intense. My brain is still trying to process everything. It felt like everything happened so fast, but it looks like the sun is about to rise," Ben says as he enters, looking at all the damage around them.

Lyra cannot believe it was morning already. She looks out the barn and witnesses, in the distance, the sunlight breaking free from the horizon. "Damn! We have to make camp here and figure out our next move."

"Wait, I've seen vampires walk around in the sun back at Hickory Lakes," Liam says, confused by everyone's hurry to make sure no light gets in the barn.

Mason takes lead on the explanation. "Our world is an air pocket dimension to the human world. The sun in our world is almost like a reflection. It doesn't hit us directly like it does to this one."

As Liam processes the information, the others waste no time. Lyra orders Mason to make sure the owners are safe and won't be a bother before they are able to move on. Ben follows the wizard as Liam helps the vampire make camp within the barn.

Lyra glances at Cedric, upset that she couldn't prevent everything from happening. For a moment, she questions her leadership. Her mind goes back to Mitch and all the dominos that fell because of that mission. "What else will go wrong now that I might be without my best friend?" she asks herself.

Mason and Ben return, informing her that the task is complete. All the windows and holes are patched up. Cedric needs medical attention, so Lyra radios her father about the situation. The walkie is a little staticky, but she eventually reaches him. Mason sits by Cedric, making sure he is stable until help arrives.

"Everyone gets some rest. The captain is sending a medical team and we are going to need all the energy we can get to finish this mission," the vampire announces. She knows her team couldn't rest. Like her, they are itching to move as soon as possible. But until then, they have to wait.

Chapter 12

Halloween morning, the sun begins lighting up the sky. Etta's driving an old pickup truck that Ian hotwired to travel back to the city. The witch is quiet during the drive as she plays back everything in her head. "Maybe I could have done something else to keep them off our backs," the witch blurts out.

Ian glances at her, displeased with her way of thinking. "You did the only thing you could do that would have worked." He watches as she torments herself thinking too much of everything. He knows that if she continues doubting herself, she won't go through with the plan. He needs to keep her focused. "So, who was that guy that was like you?"

She looks at him, "That would be my brother-in-law."

He releases a smile on his face, "Does he not want his brother back? He wouldn't help you?"

"That's complicated."

"Why?"

Etta straightens herself on her seat. "We never really got along. Mitchell had a rocky relationship with him too."

She thinks back to six years ago on Christmas Eve. The mayor at the time was having the annual *All Black with a Santa Hat* party. She was entering the ballroom with Mitch as he wore an all-black tux and her an all-black deep-v strapless gown. Everyone had on a red Santa hat and was having the time of their lives. The elegant ballroom had gold and black Christmas decorations with a hint of red. By the ten-foot Christmas tree, a live band was playing music and the wizard asked for a dance. For an hour, they danced in the dimmed-lit room. Once they were done, she left to go to the restroom to fix her makeup and when she walked out, Mitchell was talking to Lyra, Cedric, and Danny. As she approached, Mason came along and wrapped his arm around his little brother. She stopped in her tracks as she was irritated with him because every time Mason was around, trouble was not far behind.

"Oh, the old *ball and chain*, come over here and let's get this party started!" Mason called out. Mitch nudged his brother for the comment, and he apologized.

"Mase, you came. I don't think the mayor is going to appreciate having you in his home," she informed. Mitchell explained to her that he talked with the mayor and that it was ok if he kept an eye on him. The witch was annoyed with her boyfriend because he's always helping his good for nothing brother no matter the cost.

"My brother promised to be on his best behavior," Mitch informed. "I know he doesn't want Krampus after him again."

Mason scoffed. "Oh, that little devil can try."

"He did try, or do I not remember that right?" Lyra added.

Mason snatched a glass of champagne off one of the waitress trays. "Yeah, but lucky for me, I have the best brother in the world who has my back and if that guy breaks free from his cell, then he would have to face the Bettings once again!"

As Etta rolled her eyes, Mason cheered his brother by clinking his glass against his. Mitchell turned to her and said, "Hey, can I talk to you in private?"

Happy to get away from his brother, she accepted and followed him outside to the balcony. It was cold and the snow flurried in the air. He wrapped her in a big coat so she wouldn't freeze. There were a couple of people scattered around the large balcony, but they seemed to leave as soon as they walked outside.

Turning back to Mitch, she saw him down on one knee. He held her hand in his and explained to her how much she meant to him. Her stomach fluttered and her heart raced. Just thinking about that moment in the present day still has her heart race. The wizard pulled out a beautiful diamond ring and asked her to marry him. The only word that she knew at that moment was "yes". The witch repeated the word, and he slid the ring on her finger. They kissed and people clapped as she noticed that everyone was back outside. This was the best moment of her life, and she was glad that all her friends were there witnessing.

"Thief!" a voice from inside the mayor's home was heard.

As everyone looked back, security was chasing Mason through the ballroom as he changed into a cheap Santa costume with the beard hanging off his neck. He ran outside where everybody was standing and patted his brother on the back. "Congrats little brother, let me know where the bachelor party is at," he said with a wink as he leapt off the ledge. The crowd screamed as he jumped off with the mayor's priceless jewelry. A loud splash was heard and as they all looked over, they realized that he had landed in the frozen pool. Guards all surrounded the pool and jumped in to grab his body, but then noticed that the body was a fake. Bursting out of the garage, Mason stole the mayor's car as well and sped off through the gates. Etta was angry that her proposal was ruined by the wizard. Even though it was found out later that the diamond necklaces that Mason stole were actually the same ones that the legend Dracula had given to his brides that had gone missing from the museum months prior, she never let that anger towards him go.

******

"Pull over to this gas station. I need to use their phone." Ian says, waving his hands trying to get her attention.

Etta returns to reality; she pulls up to a pay phone and Ian climbs out of the truck. She sees him make a call. It takes about five minutes before he starts walking back. "So, what was all that for?" she asked.

A smile escapes his face, "I was talking to Madam Olivia Pierre-Louis, she practices voodoo in the French quarter. She knows many people who does the same and is willing to speak

166

with us about our cause."

The witch nods and shifts her eyes back on the road. Everything is moving forward, and she knows the only way to make her plan work is to recruit allies today. "Is she someone we can trust?"

Ian nods. "She is a woman of her word. When we show her what we could do for her and her people, they will all be on our side."

As they enter the city, they make their way towards Bourbon Street. Etta parks the truck, and they travel on foot. It is still early in the morning, so the streets aren't busy yet, but knowing the significance of the day and how the people of the city enjoy this specific holiday, it isn't long before things get crazy. The place is decorated from top to bottom, from skeletons hanging from the balconies to pumpkins and other seasonal themed décor spread throughout.

"This way," he directs as they turn the street corner. Flames burn bright from the lanterns hanging above them. He looks at the piece of paper that he wrote the address on and led the way. "Here we are." They walk up to the building and knock.

The door was already cracked open. Ian enters first, but before Etta could follow, the smell of smoke fills her nostrils. She looks across the street and notices smoke coming out of the alleyway, but it seems to be still. Hovering there for a bit, and then vanishing. Ian calls for her, so she just shakes off what she thought she saw and enters. Opening the door to a dim calm room, Etta steps in, analyzing the decor. There are velvet curtains along the windows with a lot of alligator statues. Her eyes start to tingle with the smell of spices in the air. Her nose gets filled with a delicious smell as she hears somebody in the back cooking.

"Excuse me but we are looking for Madam Olivia Pierre-Louis!?"

"Have a seat, I will be with you in a moment," Olivia calls out from the kitchen. After a moment of the sound of pots clinking and the water from the sink pouring, Madam Olivia Pierre-Louis walks into the room. "You must be the one's from the phone call earlier?"

Ian extends his hand to greet her, "Why yes, we have a once in a lifetime proposition for y–"

Before he could finish, Olivia interrupts, "Sorry but we don't talk business on an empty stomach." She guides them to the dining room table. "Have a seat and my daughters will serve you a hot plate."

The three of them take a seat and the delicious smell that Etta was smelling when she first walked in is finally visible. In front of her, she is plated with some grits and grillades and in the center of the wooden table is a coffee pot along with some powdered calas. Her mouth waters as the smell of the food are intoxicating. She didn't realize how hungry she was until her belly started growling. Last time she ate anything was a day and a half ago, so Etta is ready to dive right in. "Thank you for the food. I was not expecting this," she says sincerely.

Olivia smiles. "Just a little southern hospitality. My grandma always told me when we have guests over, make sure you have a hot meal ready." She takes a moment reminiscing about her time with her grandma, cooking in the kitchen for the neighborhood and being taught all her recipes. "She would always wake up before the birds and just be in the kitchen whipping up our meals for the day."

They continued eating as the room went silent. The only sound is the silverware against the plates. Ian wipes his mouth with a cloth and clears his throat, "Now about our proposal."

Madam Olivia interrupts him once more. Her eyes make eye contact with Etta. "You... I get the vibe from you that you are missing something... Someone I should say... You are heartbroken. I will trust what you have to say."

Etta felt shocked that she guessed all that just by looking at her. She started to feel as if she was an open book that everyone could read. Her eyes shift to Ian and then back at Olivia. She knows deep in her heart that this is her time to be honest. That Madam Olivia would see through the crap she would try to feed her with.

"I need to take down a powerful wizard that I believe had something to do with the death of my husband."

Olivia pauses and continues staring at Etta. Her eyes do not move away for a second. She analyzes her face closely. "And what would you expect us to do if I may ask?"

The witch leans towards her from her chair. "I have an

ancient powerful stone called the heart of mare. I just need to set it up at a safe place and activate it. Once that's done, we need to ignite the fears that humans have about voodoo. With the help of Halloween, that fear will spread, and the stone will make all of it come true. You and everyone that people believe to be witches, will gain Hollywood's version of voodoo magic and become powerful beings."

Olivia's eyes express interest. "And I'm going to assume that you would need us to channel our powers to you to be able to fight this wizard you speak of?" Etta nods her head. "If I get you the witches, will you guarantee our safety?" she asks.

The witch lays back into her chair with confidence. "If you agree, then we will be a sisterhood. All of your obstacles will be mine as well."

The two ladies stood up and shook hands. "Then a sisterhood we are," Olivia pulls Etta in closer, "but be careful of the company you keep." Her eyes shift towards Ian. "There's a reason I wanted you to be the one to talk to." Etta moves her eyes to the side, slightly looking back at Ian. They meet back looking into Olivia's eyes and she nods. "Well, looks as if I have a lot of calls to make this morning," her voice gets louder as they both turn towards the front door. Ian gets up and follows. "I will inform my people to spread the word to every man, woman and child about the great and powerful voodoo with our magic and dolls to spice up this Halloween and we will meet with you two tonight," Olivia adds.

They both say goodbye to Madam Olivia and begin

walking the road once more. Ian grabs the witch's hand, "I too have to go do my everyday duties, so for now I leave, and I will meet you again at the nearby cemetery."

"The cemetery? Why would I go there?" she asks, puzzled.

Ian gives her another smirk showing his yellow teeth. "Isn't that where the man from the club told you to go?" He pats her on her shoulder and leaves. He turns around to throw in an idea to her, "Also, tourists love going to the cemetery in New Orleans. A perfect spot to spread the word to speed up this process, don't you think?" She agrees and starts heading in that direction.

Getting to the cemetery, Etta finds a good place to activate the stone. An old crypt of a wealthy family that takes care of the tomb. She picks the lock and enters. Etta places the stone on top of a small table that is inside. The tattoo on her arm begins to glow as she ignites her wand. She twirls her hand to activate it. A repeating thumping sound is faintly heard in her ears. A red glowing light slowly flashes in the amber stone, on and off with each thump.

"So it begins," she whispers to herself.

Walking out of the crypt, the witch smells the smoke again from before. Looking around the cemetery, she investigates. Eyes are felt watching her from behind as the smoke slowly rises around her. The witch turns to the dark powerful presence. A tall man wearing an old worn-out dark suit along with black feathers mounted on his top hat with long-dreaded hair is staring at her. He has a skull painted across his face. He has a cigar in his mouth and a bottle of rum in his hand. His hat covers his eyes, and he has a snake hanging from his neck, hissing. The man takes the cigar out from between his lips and lifts his hat slightly higher on his forehead. His eyes have a yellow glow as they look straight into hers.

"You didn't tell that woman that you were trying to resurrect the man that you loved from the dead," he calmly says in his deep voice.

"Who are you?" Etta questions as her tattoo begins to glow. She doesn't know the agenda of this person, but there is a darkness about him. She can feel it.

The man stands quiet as his eyes never move away from hers. "I know what you want, and I may be able to help you out." He takes a sip from his bottle. "The way you are going, you won't be powerful enough to take out your enemies. You will fail."

"You never answered my question. Who are you?" she asks more aggressively the second time.

He smiles and with his deep calm voice says, "They call me Baron Samedi and again, you won't win."

Etta had done her research and came across chapters about Baron Samedi. He's the loa of the dead. She smelt his cigar earlier before meeting with Madam Olivia and realized he was alive before she activated the heart of mare. He's been around in the background all this time. She is intrigued about what he has to say.

"You need power that is not just from the power of the living," he pauses to blow smoke from his mouth. "You will need help from the ones that now live on the other side of the road if you know what I mean."

"And what would a being like you want in return?" she asks knowing there must be a catch. Etta thinks that there is some sort of game he's playing, but he's not showing all his cards.

Baron smirks and then begins walking closer. "There is a power that your grand wizard possesses that has me feeling a little uneasy." He circles the witch. "We have our suspicions, but if his own kind is willing to sacrifice oneself to bring an end to the madness, then I am willing to oblige."

Confused about what he means when he says *we,* she was trying to stay focused on her mission and how Baron can help. She ignores her many questions and only focuses on one. "What do you know about Gabriel that you are not telling me?"

"Don't underestimate his power. You will need to be willing to die when facing him if you have any shot at defeating him."

"Why not go against him yourself then? You and your *friends*?" she asks. "Why would I agree on putting my life in danger when you are more powerful than I am and I'm assuming the ones you know may hold such power as well?"

He inhales his cigar once more. "Because if you do... I

am the loa of the dead. If you succeed, I will help you bring your husband back from death's grips." He gets even closer to her with a more important detail, "But I will only bring one soul back, so if you shall fall on your quest but are successful, I will only bring you or your loved one back."

Etta stays quiet. She thinks about her options. Her chances of success are unknown, but the price of getting her husband back is well worth it. The witch looks back up into Baron's yellow eyes with confidence. "Give me the ritual we need to perform to get the job done so I can be with Mitchell again."

Baron Samedi smirks as he exhales, "You better not die then."

Chapter 13

Well, there goes Mr. no sleep till justice is served, Lyra thinks to herself as Liam finds a little corner to fall asleep in. The vampire keeps her eyes on Cedric until the medic arrives. Everyone is exhausted from the long night. She sends Ben out to patrol the area, so no unexpected guest shows up. Watching Cedric lying there, Lyra begins to get inside of her own head again. *I should have been there for you Ced's. Another mission and one more friend goes down under my watch.* Having doubts about her leadership, her father's request of her taking over for him when he retires plays in her head. H*ow could I lead a city if I can't even take care of my friends?*

Mason notices her struggling in her thoughts across from him. He feels as if he must talk to her at some point about everything going on, so he moves in. "Hey, you mind if I sit here?" he points at a spot beside her. She looks up at him and rolls her eyes. He waits for an answer but doesn't get one. "Ok, I'm going to sit if that's alright?" Mason crosses his legs as he sits on the floor. "I wanted to see if we could possibly talk, I've noticed you seem a little upset."

Lyra tilts her head with a sarcastic attitude, "Oh?

Detective Bettings, nothing gets past you." She crosses her arms and looks back at Cedric.

Knowing he probably deserved that, he stands silent for a second. "Look, I know you're upset. I would be upset with me as well if I were you! I would like to explain." He looks at her, but she doesn't acknowledge him. The wizard rubs the back of his neck as he exhales. Lyra is angry, but he needs to get things off his chest, so he just goes for it. "Ever since we were kids, Mitchell was always good at everything. Everything came so easily for him and for me, I had always struggled. I felt like I've always had to try harder."

Lyra slightly turns her head to listen, thinking to herself that this is the first time Mason has opened up to someone like this. She's extremely irritated at him for leaving her, but at the same time she knows that she needs this just as much as him.

"After our parents went missing, I just brushed him off and started acting out. I stopped trying. I grew frustrated and gave up!" He takes another moment before continuing, "The day he died, I felt my heart drop. I felt empty inside and a part of myself died with him." Mason's eyes look up and he sees Lyra looking at him sincerely. His eyes started to tear up. "I was hoping during the day of the dead, that his spirit along with all the others would appear and I could talk to him but when he never showed up, I just couldn't handle it."

Lyra feels his pain. She places her hand on his. "Mason, it might have been just too soon for his spirit to appear. Maybe this time we might be able to see him."

The wizard shakes his head, "I thought about that, but I needed to try to make sure nothing was wrong. I didn't want to wait a year just to find out something bad was happening to him this whole time," he explains. "I left to see if I could find something, anything to make sure. I went to places around the world that were rumored to be entrances for spirits but came out with nothing." He stands up to pace. "I couldn't come back. I was lost. He was my little brother and I was supposed to look after him, but I failed. I couldn't face everyone again, so I stayed away." Mason looks at the ink on his arm. "I didn't know what else to do so I felt like I needed to honor him somehow. He would have wanted me to better myself, so I met with a friend in London who helped me with mastering my magic. I still have to vocalize the spells that I want to do, but I'm good enough to make him proud of me."

The vampire stands up beside him. "Mason, your brother was always proud of you. He might not agree with a lot of your decisions, but he loved you."

Mason smiles at her. "Thanks, but I know I made a mistake by leaving you. I know you hate me, and I hate myself for it."

She turns around to try to explain her thoughts to him, "I don't hate you, Mason. Yeah, I was hurt. You left without saying anything to me and I felt horrible. Your brother got killed while I was there. I failed him and Etta and more importantly, I failed you." Lyra explains to him that she doesn't feel like a good leader anymore. That what just happened to Cedric is more proof to herself that she isn't suited for it anymore.

The wizard hears how she felt. "Remember the time when you came up with the idea of having me help catch the leader of the crime family in Apparition Valley? Nobody else liked the idea but you thought it would work and it did."

"Well, then you escaped after the job was done and a few months later, you came to us for help because the dragon gang in Hickory Lake's said that you snitched on them for trying to sell the mayor's painting that you sold to them week's prior."

The wizard chuckles, "Yeah, that was funny. They were short on the payment, thinking I wouldn't notice, but what I'm trying to say is that you make decisions in life and not all of them are going to have the same good outcome. Life happens and we have to learn. We could lose people anytime. We can't let our failures stop us. We learn and get better."

They both got a lot out in the open on how they are feeling, and it feels good. Even though it is just the first step of them allowing themselves to recover, it feels good having that weight lifted off them. In a moment of silence, their eyes got lost looking at the others. Lyra always had this feeling every time she looked into his brown eyes. For that moment, everything that just happened and everything they are going through has just vanished. Her heart starts pounding and from what her ears can hear, his is also. Mason moves closer to her, and she does the same. She catches his eyes moving down to her lips. Her heart races faster in anticipation as she bites the bottom of her lip. They are inches away now, but, in that moment, Lyra realizes that she couldn't hear all the snoring Liam was doing. Her eyes shift and she sees him lying forward on his elbows, feet swinging back and forth behind him as he stares at them both.

"And the moment dies," the vampire moves back, weirded out at the rookie being a creep.

Liam quickly picks himself up from the floor as he apologizes for ruining their moment, "No, no, no wait I'm sorry! I didn't mean to stare! I saw the moment you guys were sharing and it was beautiful, and I didn't want to make any noises to mess it up!"

A green light luminates from one side of the barn as a portal opens. Captain Thaddeus walks through along with a medic team following behind. Hunter leads them to where Cedric was resting. "Ms. Vansin, come here," the captain orders. Lyra walks over and looks back to see the medical team aiding her friend. "So, what are we up against?" he asks.

Lyra's eyes glance at Mason and then back to her father. "Etta took advantage of our relationship with her and made a statement that she is not messing around."

Thaddeus' face is nervous. "How are you feeling? Are you hurt?" She informs him that she is fine. That Cedric was the one who paid the price for her underwhelming leadership. "Lyra, we all make mistakes. You handled everything better than I would have. Now we must put our feelings aside and get the job done, and maybe after we have Etta, we could try and help her," he adds.

Hunter leaves Cedric and makes his way to Lyra to see if she's ok. He places his hand on the vampire's arm while talking to her. They exchange words and then he smiles at her as he walks back to the medical team.

Mason leans over to Lyra, "Who the hell is that clown?"

"That's just Hunter. While you were gone, he started working with us."

"Well, I could kick Hunter's curly headed ass," he mumbles.

"What was that?" she asks. He shrugs his shoulders and walks off.

"Isn't this just sad," Jason says as he walks through the portal. Lyra cringes as she hears his voice. Everyone looks over at him, an amused look on his face. "Looks like I missed the Nocturnal squad's famous dumpster fire of a hunt."

"Sorry Eriks, but this area is off limits. We are working on a case," Lyra informs.

Jason laughs, "Oh, well excuse me then. I'll just go inform Gabriel on what a real professional came up with for the case then."

Lyra feels annoyed by everything that comes out of his mouth but can't afford not to hear what he has to say. "Jason, what are you talking about now?"

He grins as he pulls a piece of paper from his pocket. "Well, while you guys were too busy playing cat and mouse with a little ole witch, I did real detective work and searched through her room." Jason lifts the piece of paper in the air for everyone to see. "This was found under her mattress. It seemed to be torn from a book. A book about witchcraft dolls. I realized where she ran off to and after interviewing a few witnesses from when she snuck into the library in the castle she was being held in, Etta was holding a book about Voodoo. Do you know what she intends on using this power for?"

As he was about to continue with his findings, he is met with a voice from the corner, "She's trying to use the power from the heart of mare to create witches using the local's love of voodoo. After she completes that part of her plan, she intends on using the magic to bring Mitchell back from the dead. People believe that Voodoo can make a zombie." Jason looks back with anger in his eyes and sees Cedric sitting up. "Before I turned, I overheard some guy talking to her about bringing Mason's brother back, so I thought more about what I've read at the library and there were a few mentions about zombies."

Lyra rushes over, relieved that her friend was awake. "How are you feeling?" She sits beside him, analyzing his injuries and then giving him a hug. "I'm so sorry Cedric for what happened."

Samara walks through the portal unnoticed by anyone as she has a piece of paper for the captain. She was caught off guard when she saw Cedric without a shirt. The half reptile's eyes wandered around his muscular arms from a distance. Staring at his veins, she blushes and stood off to the side as she forgot why she was there.

"Fangs, I should be sorry. I messed up by going on my own. I should've stuck to the plan." He tries standing up but realizes how hurt his body really was. "Oh, damn that's painful. Sorry I'm a little bit sore."

Lyra smiles with regret. "Sorry, but when you went full wolf on us, I may have held my punches a little less than usual."

He laughs it off and then picks himself up with assistance from his partner. Hunter walks over to give Cedric some new clothes. "Here you go buddy. Sorry, but this is all we were able to get our hands on in a short period of time."

It's a white shirt and some gray sweatpants. "Wait, where's my jacket?" he looks around the area. Mason tells him that all his clothes ripped apart during his beastly transformation. Bummed about his jacket, he sees the red plaid button down that he woke up covered in. "I could make this work."

"Wait, can we all have a wardrobe change? I'm starting to smell like a farm here," Liam asks the captain.

Thaddeus raises an eyebrow at the rookie. "Unfortunately, time isn't on our side, so we have to move. Mr. Jackson, go see if the doctor is ready with the serum." The vampire nods his head and then leaves through the open portal.

"Serum? What serum are you talking about? For what?" Lyra asks.

Captain Vansin smirks at his daughter. "For a couple of years now, the doctor has been secretly working on a serum that would allow our kind to move under the human sunlight."

Lyra was at a loss for words. She is just as excited as her father. Soon, one big weakness for her kind won't be a weakness for long. The curse of the human sun will be no more.

Dr. Stein enters with Hunter. Gabriel is seen on the other side of the rift, keeping it open for them to be able to move back and forth with ease. The doctor presses a button on his robotic torso and a compartment opens. A small vile emerges with an orange liquid substance inside. "This, my friends, is what we've been waiting for. My hard work is finally a reality." He pulls it out and hands it to the captain. "Now, this is just the beginning. It will work, but if my calculations are correct, only for twenty-four hours. Well, more or less." The vampires look at the doctor. Before they can display any concern, the doctor tells them that the serum is a guarantee. "The good news is that it will work. The bad news is that it is only for twenty-four hours. Oh, and it should take about three hours to kick in after ingesting it."

"Three hours!?" the captain questions, sounding aggravated. "We are on a time limit doctor! We don't have time to spare!" Thaddeus rubs his face with the inconvenient news.

"I have an idea sir," Mason chimes in. The captain looks at the wizard and gives him his full attention. "While Lyra takes the vile, I could take the rook into the city to see what we could find. Maybe get back on Etta's trail."

Thaddeus takes a minute to think. He glances at his daughter. "I don't know. If something happens, you two won't have any backup."

"I'll go," Cedric insists. Thaddeus denies him because of

his condition. "Captain, please. I feel fine. My head is clear and I'm ready to finish what we started."

Thaddeus looks at his daughter to get her take on the situation. She nods, agreeing with Mason's proposal. Thaddeus hesitates.

"I trust her decision completely sir," Hunter adds as he smirks at the vampire. Lyra smiles back while Mason rolls his eyes at the suck up.

With his full trust in his daughter, he agrees, "Ok, you guys can go ahead. But! If there's any sign of trouble, report in, and I will send a team in to assist."

"Or maybe captain, you should just send my team in. We could be in and out," Jason insists with confidence.

The captain denies his request, "We will let them continue their mission until further notice. But you will be the backup if anything goes wrong so have your team ready for my word."

Jason grins at Lyra as he walks through the portal. She can't believe her father would do that to her knowing they don't like each other very much. Ever since Eriks came about, there has just been bad blood between them. If her father wasn't a captain, Jason would give him an attitude too. He hated vampires ever since his parents were killed by one. Lyra looks up at her father and sees the look in his eyes, knowing he only did it to motivate them. He knows we would do anything to not be helped by Jason and his team. She looks at her team and sees on their faces that they are ready.

"Ok, let's start moving on out gentlemen," the captain announces, trying to get everyone moving.

Mason reaches his hand towards Lyra's, trying not to let the captain see them. Their eyes lock and the wizard walks out of the barn.

As Mason was about to enter the vehicle, Danny calls out for him. "Mase! You got a minute?" The wizard pulls Mason to the side "Hey man, I been wanting to talk to you for a while but never seem to have a chance."

"Yeah, what's up?" Mason gives him his full attention.

"I just want to say that I'm sorry about your brother."

"Hey, its ok. Things happen. It sucks but we all will get through."

Danny's face shows regret. "Look Mase, I was supposed to be on that mission, not your brother."

"What are you talking about?" he asked, not knowing where he was going with this.

"I was assigned to Lyras team for that assignment. I was supposed to be in Sleepy Hollow that night." He stopped to see his reaction to the news. "Right as I was making my way over to Mt. Hollow, I saw a Djinn in the woods, and she looked as if she was in an accident," Mason's eyes wandered towards the floor with the idea that his brother didn't have to be there. "I had to help her, so I pulled over to assist. She lost control of her vehicle and crashed. There was blood so I took her to the hospital. Your brother was with Lyra and Cedric, so I asked him to take my place-," he continued but didn't know what else to say. He regrets letting Mitchell go instead of himself. Like Lyra, he too had been living with guilt for the past year.

Mason saw that Danny was heartbroken with the events that occurred. He felt the pain he was feeling at that moment. He places his hands on Danny's shoulder "Hey, none of what happened is your fault. I'm not mad at you if that's what you were thinking was going to happen. Thank you for telling me but if you would have gone, you might have been killed." He gives the wizard a friendly tap on the arm, "Hey, its ok."

Danny felt a little better talking with Mason. He still felt guilty, but this chat was very much needed for him. They turned their separate ways, but Danny wanted to add one more thing. "Mase." The wizard turns around and acknowledges. "I heard you've been working hard on your magic. After you are done with your mission, maybe I can help you get better with the combat side of it."

"I'll take you up on that offer. I've heard all about the *badass* Danny Lin," he replies. He knew both Danny and Mitchell used to always train together back in the day.

The wizard joins his team in the car and drives off. Danny walks back into the barn where Lyra is about to take the serum.

"Alright now let's get this over with," she says while

reaching out for the vile. She tilts her head back and drinks it. "Oh wow, is that cinnamon I taste?"

"Yes, Frankie insisted on adding a flavor to it." the doctor explains.

Lyra smiles. "Well, tell him he will be a good bartender one day." Her skin begins to tingle. "Wait, what's happening?"

"Don't worry, this is just a minor side-effect. It just means that it is working," the doctor explains. "It will only last a minute, but you will then start to feel a little weak, so we will have to monitor you for a while to make sure everything is ok."

Hunter helps her get comfortable. "Don't worry, I'll be here the whole time." He places her where Cedric was resting. "Whatever you need just let me know." He looks into her eyes with his bright blue ones. She thanks him and then sits down.

"Lyra how are you feeling?" her father asks. He is concerned because vampires are strong creatures. They don't get sick nor have days that they felt off.

She takes a moment as she feels all her energy draining from her body. Looking up at him she replies, "Definitely weaker."

He can tell by her weary eyes that the doctor's predictions are correct. The last time he saw her this vulnerable was the day he turned her into a vampire. The doctor reassures the captain that she will be fine. That it will pass soon, and she will feel like herself in no time. Thaddeus believes him, but it was still hard to see his daughter miserable. His memories about that day flood his mind. He wasn't in time to save her mom, but he saved her and raised her as if she was his own.

"Captain Vansin," a raspy voice emerges. The vampire looks back and finds Gabriel walking through the portal. "All I've been hearing is that the witch keeps slipping through our fingers." He glances at Lyra. "I know you don't want my opinion, but I believe that we need to send another team in to obtain her?" he refers to Jason's team.

Thaddeus is annoyed that the wizard is hovering around. "Respectfully Gabriel, Lyra's team has it handled, and I don't need any advice on how to do my job, so if you would like to be so kind, go be with all of the other civilian's getting ready for all of the Halloween festivities, that would be great!"

The grand wizard became irritated. He agrees to back off and let them do what they are trained for. Gabriel glances back at Lyra and gives her a side smile. "I hope you can get this done quickly." He walks back through the portal and vanishes.

"That guy creeps me out a little," Hunter tells the captain while also keeping an eye on Lyra.

Thaddeus smirks, "He's just an old pain in the ass. He wasn't always like that though."

"Right, but that *old pain in the ass* that just left was the only one that could make a rift stable enough to walk back and forth without the whole nausea feeling," Hunter adds.

Thaddeus sighs at the fact that they now have to use a port-rift. He then begins reminiscing about the past and how things used to be with himself along with Gabriel and Mason's parents.

It isn't long before he gets interrupted by Samara who was standing in the corner, remembering why she was there and trying to find the right time to talk with him. "Captain, I know this isn't the right time, but the mayor was asking for you." She hands him the flier.

Thaddeus reads the orange paper he was given. "What is this? The Halloween Spook Festival? Why am I looking at this?"

Samara hesitates, "Th–the mayor wanted you to be present during the event. He wanted you to be seen beside him."

The vampire raises an eyebrow. He was confused about why the mayor needs him at a festival. "And why would I be there and not be handling the mission at hand? We are at a high level of threat, so I don't have time for this Spook whatever this is."

"That's why the mayor needs you there with him. People in the city are on edge and he thought with you there with him that the people would be more at ease," the half reptile explains.

"I mean, yeah I understand that," Abigail agrees. "If the people see you at the festival, then they would think the situation isn't that bad and won't panic," she explains.

Thaddeus takes a moment to think about it. "Fine! But only to prevent mass hysteria. I will show my face for a little then slip out while everyone is having their fun." He walks towards Lyra before he leaves. "I'll be back. Are you ok?"

189

"I'm slowly starting to feel better," she assures him. "I'll be fine. Go shake hands and kiss babies, ok?" she teases.

Thaddeus feels better that she still has her sense of humor. Danny activates the port-rift so the captain can meet up with the mayor. "Mr. Jackson, I'm leaving you in charge so call me if anything happens," he orders before taking off.

The young vampire agrees and then salutes the captain as he leaves. Hunter smiles at Lyra then jokes, "Well, look at me, moving up in the world. So do you call me boss now?"

Lyra gives a weak laugh, "Yeah, I don't think so. As soon as I'm one hundred percent, I'll be taking over."

Hunter laughs and stares at the vampire. Lyra notices the look he is giving, so she ends up changing the subject. "Hey, would you be able to radio Cedric? We should probably check in on them." He agrees and goes to do so. She stands up and slowly walks towards the barn's entrance where she sees some sunlight shining through. Lyra reaches her hand out to the light and holds her hand there. "Almost there. Just a little more time." She pulls her hand back and then hears Hunter on the radio. "Sounds like the boys are almost back to the city." The vampire smiles to herself as she is excited to be out in the daytime in the human world. Even if it is only for a day. She is just ready for what was ahead.

Chapter 14

Driving back into the city, the boys try to figure out where to start looking for Etta. The device Mason used the other night to search for her is still damaged. Cedric watches as the wizard tinkers with it for any chance for it to work. "I don't know man. We might have to do this the old school way of talking with some locals. See if they saw anyone that fits her description."

Mason places the device back in his bag. "We just have to think like her. If we were witches trying to use the heart of mare, what would we be doing right now?" The car becomes silent. The boys are trying to put themselves in her shoes, but no ideas are being presented.

"So, Mama-Bear, when you get out of the shower in your human form, do you smell like a wet dog or how does that work?" Liam asks while trying to break the silence. He realizes that Cedric is ignoring him. "Right, bad timing. I'll come back to that question later." They drive some more with no ideas being shared. Looking out the window, Liam sees a lady talking to a group of people while holding a doll. His mind takes a moment to process, but then an idea sparks, "You said the stone could create things that people fear right?" Everybody looks back at the rookie, agreeing with his question. "Then maybe she would be out there spreading word about voodoo to everybody!"

Ben joins in, "Right, but everyone here knows the truth about it. They won't be afraid of it because they don't believe all the crazy hype pop culture shows of it."

"The locals do, but everyone who doesn't live here believes the hype," Cedric says. "I would be targeting the tourist if I was her."

Everyone is on the same page now. "So, let's follow the tourist and maybe luck will be on our side, and we'll find her," Mason adds.

Cedric parks the car on the side of the road. They make their way towards Bourbon Street where all the tourists go when they come into town. Due to Halloween, the city is decorated heavily. Everywhere you look, there is fake blood on windows, ghosts and bones scattered throughout the French Colonial style buildings and everyone is dressed up and having a good time.

The wizard scans the block. "I guess everyone is starting early huh." Street performers are banging on buckets like drums and everyone there is dancing and partying either on the street or up on the balconies. People are in all sorts of costumes. There are humans dressed as superheroes, monsters, and characters from movies. The details people put in their costumes are amazing. New Orleans seems to be one of the top places to spend Halloween in.

Cedric talks to a lady that looks to be visiting from out of town. "Excuse me ma'am, has anyone came up to you talking about voodoo?" She response in Spanish informing him that she does not speak English.

Liam guides the wolf aside to hear what she was saying. "She's saying that they made her drink chicken blood as an initiation to their coven."

"I highly doubt she said all that," Cedric responded as he apologizes to the lady and moves the team along.

Liam hears noises coming from his stomach. "Well, I work better on a full stomach so can we stop and get a little something to eat?"

"Lucky for you guys, this city is known for its food," Ben calls out from Mason's bag. A lady walking by hears him and is startled.

"Right, let's get something quick, but Ben you need to be quiet right now. Humans can hear you buddy," he informs the ghost as he releases a friendly smile to the lady while swinging the bag to his other shoulder. "Ok, so what should we get?"

"Is it too early for some seafood?" Cedric throws out with a huge smile on his face.

Mason chuckles, "That sounds amazing, but unfortunately we need something to grab and go right now."

The boys look around to see if they find something. Even though Ben knows he had to be quiet, but he just couldn't help himself, "Guys c'mon, grab some coffee and beignets." The group glances at each other with eyes wide open in agreement.

Noticing an old man staring at Mason's bag, the wizard moves the team along before they freak anybody else out.

Walking a few blocks, they reach Cafe Du Monde and finally get something to eat. They find a corner away from the crowd and Liam watches Cedric shake the bag so all the powder could stick on the beignets. He takes a bite. "Oh my gosh this is heavenly." Nothing but silence hovers over them as they eat and sip their coffee. Liam finds his moment, "So, about that wet dog question…"

"You gentlemen seem to be enjoying what New Orleans has to offer," a voice interrupts. The boys turn around to see a woman standing next to them. They feel awkward with their mouths stuffed and powder all over their faces and shirts. "My apologies, you folks seem to be enjoying them beignets," she continues.

Mason scrambles to wipe the powdered sugar off his mouth. "Sorry about that. But yes, we are. Amazing these little things are. I'm sorry but do we know you?"

The lady laughs and waves her hands. "Oh no, I'm sorry. I just saw your costumes, so I walked over. My name is Madam Olivia Pierre-Louis, and I must say, I enjoy your outfits. Are you supposed to be a masked officer?"

Everybody looks over to Liam. "Uh, sort of. I'm the invisible man that used to be a cop before the incident but now is a vigilante hero."

"Oh, how fun. Very creative," she giggles. Olivia looks

over at Cedric. "And you?"

Cedric quickly tries to think of something. He looks down at his baggy sweatpants, "Well, I don't have my makeup on, but I'm a break-dancer."

Olivia hears a snicker come from Mason. "You must be one of those lead singers from boy bands. My daughter loves them."

They all laugh at the wizard as he tries to come up with his look. "What? No! Uh, I'm a... Ugh yeah, I'm a boy band singer."

Liam and Cedric tease him and then Olivia hears another sound from Mason's bag. She examines it with her eyes until she feels them about to leave. "Wait! Aren't you going to ask what I am?" The guys look at each other and then ask what she was dressed as. "I am a voodoo queen." They trade glances with each other again. "Do you know about voodoo witches?" she asks.

Mason quickly catches on to what she is trying to do, but continues playing along, "A little bit. Don't they curse people and take control of them with dolls and pin their eyes out?"

Olivia smiles. "Yeah, they do that too," she says, looking into the eyes of each one of them. "They are dangerous if they work together. They could do all sorts of magic with the help of their dead. Harnessing their powers, they could conjure all sorts of things." She leans in closer. "Halloween time is where they have a little more fun. Especially with *out-of-town folks*."

Mason tries to act scared to sell it to the witch. The others realize what Mason is trying to do but they also are nervous about the dangerous game he's playing. They did not know when the power of the stone would kick in and many things could go wrong.

She looks down at Mason's bag again. "Would you fellas like to see my shop just down the street? Don't worry, I'm harmless."

Both Cedric and Liam agree that they are too busy to go anywhere with her, but Mason has other plans. "I'm down for it." The others look at the wizard as if he was insane. "C'mon guys, we're in New Orleans! Voodoo stuff is on the bucket list, right?" They hesitate but eventually agree to go with Olivia. She grins and then leads the way.

Following a stranger, they had only just met, Ben starts feeling a little off. "Hey Mase, something is wrong."

The wizard slips to the side of a building as the others continue walking. "What's wrong?" He opens his bag to let the ghost out. He examines him. "Oh no, I thought it would take longer for this to happen."

"What? Longer for what to happen?" Ben asks. Worried about what was happening to him and the fact that Mason knows what was wrong just by looking at him makes the ghost feel more nervous.

"There's no need to panic yet, but a spirit that doesn't crossover to the afterlife does eventually become corrupted. You will lose all memories of yourself and only live off your basic instincts. You will start to feel lonely, then fear will take over your mind. After that you will go mad then become vengeful," Mason explains.

Shocked with this new detail, Ben begins to panic. "Wait what!? Oh my god, I can't breathe! I already can't remember my past life! It had already started! I'm fading away!"

The wizard tries to calm him down. "Ben, look at me ok!? First off, spirits can't breathe. Also, we still have time to get you back to where I found you and you can still crossover before any of that happens, alright?" He reassures his friend. "The process takes time. After we are done here, I promise you, we will get you back. You might just feel some of the effects now but there is no need to panic."

Ben slowly starts to calm down. He's still nervous at the possibility of losing himself, but he believes in his new friend. "Alright Mase, I can do this."

"Thank you, Ben." He opens his bag for the ghost to hide in once more. Mason zips the bag and catches up with his team. The street they are on seem quiet. In the distance, he hears music from where all the humans are at. "How much further?"

Olivia looks back and smiles as they reached their destination. "It wasn't that bad of a walk now, was it?" She opens the door and lets them in.

"Somebody might be a little obsessed with reptiles if you asked me," Liam says, noticing all the alligator decor around the room.

"As a child, my father always took us to the Bayou. I always loved them. A predator that has patience. When their prey was caught off guard, they would strike," she explains.

"I'm having a bad vibe here man," Cedric whispers to Mason. The wolf is on his guard as the wizard walks around the room to see if he finds anything that can help them with their assignment.

"Well, gather around so we can begin," Olivia announces. She sits at the head of the table as the others come along. When everyone sat down, she instructed them to close their eyes. "Clear your minds as I summon the witches from the other side to appear."

Cedric turns his armband on to five percent so he can sense the room. When the wind begins blowing indoors, his ears catch sounds of motors from fans within the walls. He also hears somebody in the back room adjusting the lights for the theatrical effects. *Oh lord, this is how they are making people believe?* he thinks to himself, amused. Suddenly his worries settle. The wolf isn't nervous about any of it anymore. *This is all just a show.*

As Olivia begins speaking Creole louder, the wind picks up. She opens one eye and sees that they all have their eyes shut. The witch signals for her daughters and everyone else in the back to emerge. Cedric picks up on the footsteps, but it was too late.

Mason opens his eyes and sees Olivia standing up. He looks around and realizes that they are surrounded by a bunch of strangers holding hands and chanting. The wizard feels like he is wearing invisible chains, so he quickly stands up and tries to ignite his wand. Every time it seems to appear, his wand vanishes.

While Mason is struggling to keep his wand ignited, Cedric turns his arm tech on to thirty percent, but he too is struggling. Their chanting makes his tech dead.

Spirits begin to appear around them, chanting with the living witches. Olivia grabs Mason's bag and spills a powdered substance inside that makes Ben jump out and panic, not knowing what was happening.

"My eyes! My head!" he yells as he flies around the room. Whatever the substance was, it seems to be making Ben remember more than just his name. All his memories are flooding in all at once, so he feels overwhelmed with it all. He sees what he did for a job, where he used to live, where his body was at rest. *The cemetery!* The spirit remembers where his body is buried and quickly flees the scene.

"Ben, wait!" Mason calls out, but the spirit was already gone. Liam turns invisible without a word. "Cedric, go after Ben!" the wizard orders. The wolf refuses to leave him behind, but he insists as he is starting to summon the wand in his hand. Cedric sees him getting control of his magic and the power on his armband coming back on. They know they can get out of the pickle they are in.

Olivia tries to get the other witches to focus harder since their magic isn't going to hold for long, but Mason isn't going to let them win. The spirits begin fading away so the wizard yells as he ignites the energy wand and casts a shield between him and the witches. While holding the spell as strong as he can, Olivia is having her people surround the wizard. Before they all could, Liam appears out of thin air and sprays a fire extinguisher at them. This distracts them from the spell, and helps Mason get to full strength. The wizard shoots a bolt from his wand at the upper floor of the building, collapsing it so they can get away.

"Holy crap that was intense!" Liam shouts as they run outdoors. He looks back and sees that nobody was chasing them. "Sorry but I need to slow down a bit. I'm starting to get a little cramp on my side."

Mason takes him in an alley for a breather. "That was crazy. Thanks for having my back rook."

Liam lifts his head up while trying to catch his breath. "Always Mase. We're a team."

He nods at him and then looks at his tattoo. "Looks like the stone is beginning to work."

Liam picks himself up. "Was that what was happening? I thought you were having a performance issue."

"What? No! Working together like that just made them strong."

The invisible man places his hands on his hips. "Hey dude, it's ok. We all go through it at some point in our lives. No shame in not getting it up."

The wizard instantly ends the conversation there. "You just had to make things weird." He looks around the corner and sees no sign of anyone following them. He radios Cedric to get his location. "Are you there? Where are you guys?"

Nothing but static through the radio. He tries again, but still nothing. Liam helps by running through the streets, asking anyone who may have seen anyone matching his description. Empty handed; they continue trying the radio again.

With a humming tune bleeding through the radio, Cedric answers *"Mase! I'm here! I followed Ben to the cemetery! Hurry over!"*

Liam expresses his uncertainty with the idea, "Great, heading to a cemetery on the day of Halloween. Awesome."

"New Orleans cemetery? Another bucket list," Mason jokes as he was just relieved that everyone is ok. "Let me just inform Lyra so she could meet us there."

Chapter 15

Hexington Falls, along with all the other cities in Purgintor, loves this time of year. Halloween is the biggest holiday celebrated. From September through the last day of October, events and traditional activities happen across the city. From the season opening of the popular sport, Pumpkin Smash, and outdoor horror movie nights by the campfire to the major event on Halloween night. On October 31st, the town celebrates the night with a *Spook festival*. They have pumpkin carving competitions, inflatable costume racing and a parade that marches through the streets. The mayor makes sure to have his schedule cleared to enjoy the occasion.

"Captain Vansin, I'm glad you were able to join us with everything that's been going on. I appreciate your help keeping the citizens' minds at ease," the mayor greets.

Thaddeus walks in with Abigail to help him through it. He gives a fake smile. "Mayor Miller, it is always a pleasure to be here. Now if you don't mind, I have important matters to attend to so let's get on with it."

Mrs. Willows nudges the captain's arm. "I'm sorry,

Thaddeus only has his mind on work these days. No time for fun."

Mayor Harold Miller smiles as he pats the vampire on the back, "And that's why I love this guy, looking out for our streets. We can always count on him to keep the peace. He makes my job for the past two years of being the mayor of this wonderful city, easy." He takes a sip of his champagne and then hurries to greet more people as the festival begins.

"I don't have time for this. My daughter is trying out a groundbreaking serum and we still have Etta running about. I should be there with all my men," he mumbles at Abigail. He looks out at the crowd. There is a fun atmosphere spread across the town, but it was hard for him to enjoy himself when duty calls.

Abigail tries to get him through the event. "Look, all we have to do is make sure that you are seen by the public, wave to everyone from a float and we will be back in no time."

The captain agrees but his mind was still on the job, "Right! I'm just going to call Mr. Jackson to make sure everything is alright."

"Captain, just try to look as if you are enjoying yourself. People can read faces so relax and follow my lead," the shapeshifter insists.

Abigail escorts Thaddeus to Harvey's costume shop where a few people are out celebrating. Some of them are owners of shops and bars. He shakes hands and makes his rounds, making sure he is seen. She even gets his picture taken with the mayor by the Hexington Daily News company. Willows makes sure to cross her T's and dot her I's while they are there.

The mayor's assistant walks up, escorting Gabriel to get in the photo with them. Thaddeus raises his eyebrow. "What is he doing here? Is he going to try to harass me here too?"

"Well, you did tell him to come over here and enjoy the festivities," Abigail reminds.

"Captain Vansin, I assume that you have everything under control?" Gabriel asks. The captain nods, assuring him that it is. "Glad to hear it. When she is caught, I would like her to be contained in my facilities at Sacred Hills."

Thaddeus is surprised by his demands. "When we capture her, *we* will keep her in our custody for questioning!"

The vampire is stern with his decision and the wizard knows he will have issues having Etta back under his care. "This would be considered a wizard's matter so she would need to be looked after by her own kind and not by night walkers as yourself."

"Well, we shall see now, won't we?" The captain does not break eye contact with Gabriel. He wants to remind him that he is in charge here and that it was Gabriel who looked for his help with the situation.

"I hope both of you are playing nice now," mayor Harold interrupts. He signals a photographer to take a picture of all of them together. After they are done, the mayor grabs Thaddeus and walks with him towards the floats for the parade. "Ok Vansin, after this part, you can go back to work. I think we were successful here. Don't you agree?"

The float they board looks like a giant Jack-O-Lantern that has flames burning from the top. The marching band in front of the vehicle begins marching and security moves along the side. Thaddeus and Abigail look out into the crowd and see a bunch of orange and black balloons and confetti being thrown about. He looks back at the stage where they were taking pictures and still sees Gabriel looking from the distance. They make eye contact for a second and then he lifts his hood over his head and walks off.

"Thaddeus, you have to wave back at the crowd too, you know." Abigail snaps him back from his gaze.

"Right, my apologies," he mumbles. He waves and helps throw candy into the crowd. He catches the mayor laughing and having a good time on the other side of the float. When he looks back in the crowd, he sees somebody in a blood-colored cloak wearing a bronze skeleton mask with a matching crown molded on the forehead. He adjusts his eyes to get a better look. "What the hell? No, impossible."

"What's wrong?" Mrs. Willows asks. She follows his eyes and sees the figure amongst the people. "Wait, that's not what I think it is, right?"

The vampire jumps down from the float and wastes no time reaching the spot where the mystery person was standing. "He was just here!" He looks around and then looks up towards

Abigail to see if she has eyes on the person, but no luck on her end.

The shapeshifter leaps off the float and runs towards Thaddeus. "That looked like a follower for...," She dared not to finish her sentence. Abigail looks into his eyes hoping she was mistaken, but she knows deep down that she is right.

"Yes, Mrs. Willows, that seemed to be somebody, at least dressed up like one of those wretched people," he says.

She still can't believe it. "Maybe some kid is playing a horrible prank?"

He grabs her hand and makes their way back on the float. He tries calling Hunter but doesn't get an answer. "I have to go. Just in case something bigger is in play here."

As he tries to slip away, he hears a voice calling to him, "Captain! Captain Vansin! I need to speak with you!" The photographer from the Hexington Daily News is trying to push his way through the crowd to get to him. "Captain Vansin, I need to show you something!"

Thaddeus tries to ignore him. "I'm sorry, but I have important matters to attend to if you be so kind." Not wanting to take any more pictures, he declines to speak with him.

The photographer insists that he should speak to him. "Captain, this is urgent! Please give me two seconds to show you something."

Abigail convinces the vampire to speak to the goblin.

"Alright, you have one second and that's all I will be giving you."

The goblin lifts his camera over his head and clicks a button on the screen. "Look at the picture."

Both Thaddeus and Abigail look at what is displayed on the screen. All they see is just the picture he took of him with the mayor and Gabriel. "What? Looks to me, everyone's eyes were open. Thank you for showing me that. Good day." He walks away at a faster pace.

"No sir, look closely at the grand wizard!" he calls out. The photographer sees that he got the captain's attention after he stops dead in his tracks.

Thaddeus turns his head to the side, looking from the corner of his eyes at the goblin. "Show me," he orders in a calm but deep tone. Enough for the photographer to hear him.

Abigail looks at the captain's face as the goblin makes his way over to show him the photo once more. She's worried about what they are about to see. Looking down at the photo, they zoom in on Gabriel. "Who is that next to him?" Abigail asks.

The captain's eyes widened. "No, he wouldn't dare!" The figure standing next to Gabriel is a faded blue being. Studying it closely, he realizes it is a spirit that seems to be attached to him.

Mrs. Willows is baffled. "I don't understand. We made it illegal to summon ghosts with the fact of what could happen to them if they don't cross over for a certain amount of time."

"Should I inform the mayor sir?" the goblin asks.

"No!" he shouts while forgetting that people are around. He lowers his voice and orders, "You will tell no one about this. Only keep it within the three of us, do you understand?" The cameraman nods nervously. "Good, now send me this to my email asap and see if you catch anything else on those photos of yours."

The vampire begins to make his way back to where he was going. Abigail follows while trying to match his speed. "Why would he have a spirit around him?"

"I don't know but we will keep this on the hush until we figure it out. This has the possibility of being something huge, so we must make sure," he explains. "Looks like your theory about Gabriel might be correct."

The librarian agrees and they make their way outside of the city. A few security vehicles are waiting there to pick the captain up and escort him back to Mt. Hollow. The wind is picking up. Leaves scatter across the floor. The vehicle proceeds towards Mt. Hollow. The captain feels something familiar with the blurry figure in the photo but could not put his finger on it. He will keep that feeling to himself for now until he figures it out. He looks back at the city as darkness quickly hovers above. Something is about to happen.

Chapter 16

Memories flash in Ben's mind. It's like someone is trying to shove every single moment from his past back into his brain. Struggling to focus on just one, a major picture pops out the most. *Saint Louis Cemetery?* So many flashbacks keep running through his mind and trying to focus on one is like watching only one blade spinning around on a fan. *Why was the name of a cemetery highlighted above the rest?* he thought as he tries to stop his head from spinning. The spice that Madam Olivia Pierre-Louis poured on him had done something to his mind to have him start remembering things. Ben tries to push all of his energy on focusing on the cemetery. He looks more into it, trying to put pieces together. He follows his memories through a few graves until it stops at a certain crypt. He is shocked by what he saw. "Benjamin Owens? That's my name! That's where my body is!"

He explodes out of Mason's bag and rushes towards the door. As he rapidly flies out of the building, he startles a couple that was strolling down the road. Ben notices them looking up at him from the floor with their eyes in horror at what they were witnessing. Wasting no time on being discreet amongst the humans, he hurries down the block, letting the couple's presence slip his mind as quickly as he was moving.

Cedric sprints outside and sees Ben moving. Noticing the people on the ground, the wolf helps them up to their feet. "Sorry, just testing a hologram for tonight," he lies and then races off, following the spirit.

The two races through the city with Ben leading and Cedric trying to catch up. The spirit has the advantage of being able to move through solid objects. The shortcuts he makes, moving through walls of buildings, has Cedric falling behind more and more. Sliding across hoods of cars and dodging crowds of people, Cedric is drawing attention to himself from the locals.

Ok, I need to take myself away from eye level, he thinks to himself as he pushes a button and adjusts the level of his armband. His eyes turn yellow, and his nails become claws. The wolf launches himself on top of the nearby building and travels amongst the rooftops. His sharp eyes catch a view of Ben, and he is back on track.

Back at Olivia's, Mason and Liam find themselves playing catch up. The wizard calls Lyra with his commlink. He informs her of the situation and then proceeds with the knowledge of the vampire's progress with being able to walk within the sunlight. They head over towards the crowded block. Mason leads the way scanning for a way to the cemetery.

"This way! Try to keep up, rook!"

Cedric finds the ghost entering the cemetery with the feeling that he had reached where he was fleeing to. He enters slowly, not wanting to startle him. "Ben? Where are you?" he calls in a low, calm voice. The wolf passes between many crypts in search of the spirit. After a dozen tombs, he finally finds him.

Ben is standing in front of a crypt, staring at the fresh bricks that sealed the entrance. He stays quiet. Not moving. The spirit just stands there as if he is waiting for something to happen. "This is where I lay," he informs Cedric, feeling his eyes staring at him from behind. "My memories showed me this. My...my body is... here."

Cedric walks up to Ben, but before he gets close, the spirit dives inside of the crypt. Shocked at what happened, he hears footsteps that make him look back. Mason approaches. "What the hell just happened? Where did he go?"

The wolf doesn't know what to say, "His body, he just-"

Before he can continue, they hear a faint banging within. They stop and cautiously move towards the tomb. The banging is heard again, so Liam places his ear against the bricks. "Ben!? Is that you?"

"I'm alive!" a voice said from behind the bricks. "Get me out of here!" Ben yells louder as he continues to bang some more.

"He needs help! I heard him say help! We got to get him out of there!" Liam shouts while trying to kick the tomb open with his foot.

Cedric was about to switch on his wolf abilities until Mason steps forward. "Stand back! We're about to disturb the peace!" The wizard ignites his wand and shoots a bolt of lightning at the crypt entrance. With a loud explosion, the wall shatters open with dust bursting around them and pieces of bricks tumbling around the floor.

Coughing with all the dust in the air, Ben's voice is loud as he is freaking out with all the noise. Cedric quickly runs in and grabs the coffin where the banging was coming from and pulls it out. "Ben, are you ok!? Are you stuck?"

Liam reaches down to open the coffin, but instead the casket flies wide open revealing a human form of Ben.

"I'm alive!" Back in his own flesh, he struggles while wearing a tight suit that is ripping apart with each movement. The body rolls out and he struggles to get up to his feet like a calf after it's born. "Holy crap! Do you see this!?"

Cedric looks at Mason, shocked. "Mase, do you see this!?"

The wizard analyzes the situation. "I mean, he is a ghost and ghosts are able to possess bodies." He gives Ben a hand, helping him catch his balance. "This is crazy. I've never seen something like this before."

Liam is happy that everyone was taking it lightly but is unable to contain a certain issue. "So, are you a zombie?" Cedric looks at Ben once more as Liam asks his silly questions. "Do you eat brains now?" Mason and the wolf quickly step back with caution of the idea.

Ben looks down at his stomach, then looks at each of his

friends. He thinks to himself as he tries to feel what he was craving. "I... I don't know. I don't really feel hungry for anything." As his mind wonders, more memories flood his mind. He catches himself as he begins remembering things about who he was. Flashing before his eyes, as if he is watching a movie play in fast-forward, he gets glimpses of a house. He focuses on the house and in seconds he sees a portrait of himself standing with three other people. Ben can't make out who they are, so he tries harder to unblur their faces.

Cedric knows they must hurry and flee the scene after all the noises they had made a bit ago. People heard the commotion and the wolf started hearing sirens in the distance. "Guys, we have to go!" He calls out to Ben, but his eyes are shut with movement under his lids so he knows the now possessed body can't hear him.

Mason is distracted by a feeling nearby, a strong energy somewhere close. He stares at the direction where the energy is coming from, but then interrupted by Cedric pushing against his shoulder to snap out of it. "What? Uh yeah, we got to move," he says while shaking the feeling off.

Ben recognizes the faces he saw in his thoughts. "My family. My Family!" He starts to remember everything a lot easier now. His family, home, job, and everything else he ever knew. "I got to go to my wife. My daughters!" He starts running off once again, leaving everyone behind.

"Ben, wait! Let's take this one step at a time before we do anything crazy!" Mason calls out. It was no use because he was already far away.

"That zombie can run. Ugh, I hate running zombies" Liam blurts out.

Trying to catch up, NOPD storms the cemetery to locate where the disturbance took place. The boys quietly slip past them to not get caught. They sneak past a few officers as they make their way to the exit to chase after Ben.

Miles away, he runs and shows no signs of slowing down. Ben is on a mission, and nothing is going to stop him until he sees his family again. He is trying to still get used to his body again as he stumbles a few times. The zombie darts into a neighborhood and after a few houses, he stops in front of one. He watches the two-story second empire architectural style home from the yard. Seeing movement within, he runs up on the porch. Peeking into the window, he sees his family. He is scared to knock on the door, so he stands by the window.

The others catch up with Ben and see him by the house. Moving around the Halloween decorations in the yard, they meet him near the window as they gaze inside to see what he was looking at. They see his wife along with his two daughters. One is twelve years old while the oldest is sixteen.

"I died," Ben's voice cracks as he speaks. Tears begin dripping down his cheeks. "I left my family."

He gets another flashback; this time it was form last month. A vision of himself performing the cover song Time is Running Out by Muse at a bar with his band. Ben played the guitar while his wife, Jennifer, watches from a table nearby. After they were done, Ben met his wife at the bar where she looked beautiful. She was wearing a red cocktail dress with her dark wavy hair hanging down by her shoulders. He sees them enjoying themselves with their friends, drinking and dancing. Late at night, they were walking towards their car that was parked at the side of the road. Tires were squeaking in the distance when he noticed a car moving from side to side at a high speed. Ben saw his wife crossing the road as the vehicle approached. He quickly pushed her out of the way and braced himself for impact. The guy swerved his car and smacked into Ben. He flew and landed by the edge of the sidewalk where his head banged against with force. He blacked out while he heard his wife screaming for him.

After the memory finished, Ben slowly raises his arm and feels the back of his head with his fingers. He feels the wound where his head met the concrete.

As he looks back in the window, he sees his oldest daughter, Devin, talking to her mother. "No mom, I said I didn't want to do it anymore! Tell them that I'm still saying no."

Jennifer is upset. "You've worked so hard for the talent show at the fall festival. You can't let what happened stop you. Your father wouldn't want you to quit."

"Yeah, well my dad isn't here! Some idiot made sure of that!" Devin yells with her eyes starting to tear up. She throws her purse at the wall and falls on the couch.

Heartbroken seeing her daughter still mourning her

father's death, she takes a seat next to her. "Hey, I miss your father too, baby. I know we're all still healing but I also know that you and your father practiced day and night for this show. But, if you are not ready, then we could try for next year because you know he would have wanted you to do it." They both hug, comforting each other in their moment of darkness that the month had brought them.

"Today is her talent show," Ben mumbles to himself. "She wanted to be like Demi Lovato. We practiced so hard for her solo," he speaks slightly louder. He places his hand against the glass. "I'm going to find my way back to you, my loves."

Lyra walks up from behind as she watches. Rubbing his back she asks, "Are you going to be, ok?" He turns around and hugs the vampire in a tight grip. A tear drips down her face. "I'm so sorry Ben."

"We should get out of here before anybody sees us," Mason informs. They let Ben get one more look before they leave. The others begin moving out while the wizard waits for his new friend. "When all this is over, I'll do whatever I can to get you back to your family again." Ben places his hand on the wizard's shoulder, thanking him. Mason doesn't know exactly what he is going to do or where to even start, but he is going to try.

Lyra gets everyone into the car that she took. "Ok, so where do we go now?"

Everyone thinks to themselves, but none of them know where to start. Mason remembers what happened to him near

Ben's grave. "To the cemetery." They all look back at him, looking for a reason why. "While we were there, I felt something. Something powerful. Something unnatural. Must be the energy radiating from the stone," he explains.

"Then the cemetery it is," Lyra agrees. She puts the car in drive and proceeds towards their destination. Everyone seems a little off from the recent events but knows that they need to get their heads back in the game. This is it. This is where the showdown with Etta begins, and they are prepared.

Chapter 17

Following a loud explosion coming from the cemetery, the local police department is notified and incoming. Etta is not too far from the site, so she rushes over to see if the heart of mare is in danger. Making her way through the cemetery, she sees her friends with what seems to be a corpse coming out of its casket. The witch is worried when she sees Mason looking her way. She hides behind a crypt, hoping the wizard didn't see her. The sound of sirens sounds like they are just outside the walls.

Great, the last thing I need right now, she thinks to herself. Looking around at the mess they made, she tries to think of something. *If they see all of this, it will become a crime scene and they won't leave until they investigate which could take all night.* The witch continues to come up with a plan. The heart of mare can't be moved at this point because it would ruin the spell. She peeks around the corner and sees them running from the scene. An idea comes to her. *I must cloak the area, so they won't be able to see it.*

She summons her wand and casts a cloaking spell to cover the mess. Right when she did, cops swarmed the cemetery. NOPD runs through to find where the explosion happened, but they can't find anything. Confused by the 911 call, they look around a bit more. "Might have been a Halloween prank call," one of the officers says. They did one more sweep of the place and within minutes, they left.

As Etta takes down the spell, a voice comes about, "That was a close call." Madam Olivia walks out from behind a tomb. "Looks as if your stone is working. I could feel the magic running through my body."

Etta smiles, leading her to where she placed the stone. Unlocking the iron door of a crypt, Olivia witnesses the heart of mare. More witches come about, one by one to meet Etta. In just moments, the stone will complete its task and they will be able to move on to the next step of Etta's plan.

Clearing his throat from around the corner to get Etta's attention, Ian pulls out an old piece of paper. Etta meets him where the other witches can't see him. He grins at her. "I found something that may be worth a look." Ian holds the piece of paper between his two fingers.

Etta takes it and opens it. She reads the spell that was written on it and looks up at the homeless man. "Will this work?"

Ian grabs the paper from her. "This right here will make you and your new coven extremely powerful."

She thinks to herself again. Reading the spell over and over, she agrees, "I'll do it. But do you think the others can master this spell in such a short amount of time?"

Ian nods his head, informing her that the adjusted plan

will work. "They just have to chant these few words over and over and you do most of the work. This would be first grade magic for them."

Interested in how much he knows about magic and spells, Etta knows that she will have to do what she can now and figure out Ian later. She brings the new spell to the newer witches and tells them to practice. Sensing a familiar cigar smell rising, Etta knows who that could be. "You showed up."

Baron Samedi walks out of the fog. "I must admit, I'm impressed. I did not think you would be able to pull it off." He places the cigar back in his mouth. "You got the witches that you needed and soon the stone will complete its magic and you could carry on your mission."

Etta studies the Ioa of the dead. "And I would be able to take out Gabriel for you and all of your...*friends*. Then you will bring back Mitchell for me?" The witch gazes at his face.

Samedi stokes the snake that is hissing around his neck. "Of course. That is our arrangement." He takes a sip of the spiced rum from the glass bottle. "Are you having second thoughts?"

She shakes her head. "I'm only making sure that when this is done, you will hold up your end."

He smashes his bottle off to the side with anger. "I will not have my words be put into question!" The yellow shade of his eyes grows brighter. The python around his neck makes a vicious hiss, warning her. Baron Samedi calms himself down as he looks down at the unfortunate waste of rum on the ground. "If you disrespect me again little girl, you will be joining your husband."

The witch understands. "I meant no disrespect. This past year has made me a little short on trust."

He adjusts his posture and looks up at the evening sky. "The sun will set in a few hours. Make sure your witches don't screw up the spell I gave you." He tips his hat and then vanishes in the fog.

Ian watches as she returns to the other ladies to help them get ready for the night by teaching them the new spell. He glances at his watch, watching the hands tick. He makes his leave until the moon rises.

The New Orleans witches practice for hours, their brains absorb the Creole text of the spell. Practicing over and over as they feel their magic grow from the stone. They are getting stronger by the minute. The sky is a fiery orange shade. The flames from the torches Etta set around the cemetery flicker on simultaneously. The power from the stone is complete.

Etta gathers the witches in a circle as she stands in the middle. They hold hands and begin chanting. A fog flows in as they are beginning the spell. Baron Samedi appears from the smoke and watches closely. He walks closer, making his presence known by Etta. She glares at him with a menacing look.

Samedi listens closely as he hears the words leaving their lips. "Etta, that's not the spell I gave you!" he yells. He scowls at her with his eyes.

The ladies are frightened at first, but they continue chanting while others start banging on instruments. The flames around them grow as the chanting gets faster and louder. Surrounding them are witches from the dead, appearing across the cemetery.

Baron Samedi sees all the translucent apparitions all over the place, joining in the chant. He notices that the dead are transferring their powers to the living. "Etta, what are you trying to do!? We had an arrangement!"

She opens her eyes and meets his. Reaching her hand towards him as her tattoo illuminates, the witches' hands part, and the circle opens where Samedi is standing. The spirits standing behind Samedi block him from getting away. Etta has fire in her eyes. "Sorry, like I said before, I'm a little short on trust. Don't worry though, I have other plans for you."

He smirks while opening a new bottle of rum. The Ioa of the dead takes a sip and wipes his mouth. He looks into her eyes. "You better hope I never get free because I have a special spot for you on the other side, Etta." Closing his eyes and accepting his fate, his body lights up in a bright white light then gets absorbed within Etta.

Hearing his voice in her head, Etta knows that her body is not powerful enough to keep such power. "Close the circle!" The witches hold hands once again, but this time the spirits join, forming an outer circle around them. "Get ready!" she yells, preparing them for the power she will be distributing between all of them.

Dust picks up as the wind blows in a circular motion. A bright orb forms above Etta's chest causing a humming noise. Beams of light scatter out, piercing into each witch's body. The power from Baron Samedi is too great for one person, but sharing the power among others is possible. The flames from the torches shoot straight up into the sky and then die. For a moment, there is complete darkness throughout the graveyard. They all stand together in silence. A flickering begins on one of the torches. One by one, each torch begins to light up again.

Etta opens her eyes. She looks around at each face that followed her there tonight. The spirits vanished as their spell worked. She catches Ian standing by one of the crypts with a smug face, nodding his head.

"Did the spell work then?" one of the witches' questions. By the look on their leader's face, they know the answer.

Madam Olivia Pierre-Louis stands beside Etta. "So, what's next on our agenda?"

The witch ignites her wand and points it away from the group. "It's time for us to settle a score." Ian tosses a port-rift on the ground by the witch. She begins casting another spell by moving her wand in a circling motion. A green spark begins to form as she is about to open a portal to Hexington Falls. Etta believes nobody would be able to stop her until she hears a voice from behind.

"Etta!"

Chapter 18

"Oh my god! Traffic sucks! The parade is about to start, and we've been stuck on this same street for an hour!" Lyra says as roads are being blocked off in the downtown area. She gets everyone out of the vehicle. "Guess the rest of the way is on foot guys. Let's go!"

The team follows the vampire down the road. The streets have gotten more crowded with everyone celebrating Halloween. Everyone is in costume and ready for the city's annual holiday parade. Local law enforcement is scattered around the area for the night, so doing anything that would attract attention wouldn't be ideal. Even though the stakes are high, you can't help but feel the excitement from all the energy coming off everyone.

"Ok, so next week I'm just going to take a few days off and come here and actually enjoy this city," the wizard announces. Cedric agrees to join him on vacation. "Maybe Samara would like to come too," Mason adds.

The wolf releases a nervous chuckle. "I don't know. Maybe a little too much for a possible first date."

Lyra chimes in, nudging him on the arm, "Well, you have

a week to ask her on a date then to a weekend getaway. Simple."

While the team continues teasing Cedric about his love life, an unexpected voice appears, "There goes those Nocturnal Squads." Being interrupted, they look to see Jason and the Phantom Squad walking up. "We've been waiting for you guys. Seemed as if you got a little off track, didn't you?"

Lyra rolls her eyes. "Sorry, but the contest for the dumbass costume awards is in the other direction. If you hurry, I think you could still make it."

The phantom laughs. "Oh, that was hilarious, but do you want to hear something else funny? The mayor assigned us to accompany you guys to make sure the job gets done. Looks like we're going to hold your hand to the finish line sunshine."

The vampire couldn't believe it. "What!? What did Captain Vansin have to say about this arrangement?"

Proud that he was getting under her skin, Jason, in a cocky tone, replies, "Daddy had no say. After giving this trainwreck of a team a thousand chances in the past, people were already getting fed up. Now, let's not make things harder and just follow my lead."

The nocturnal squad ignores his remarks and walks right past him. They are assigned a mission, so they are going to make sure they get the job done. Lyra isn't going to let Jason and his goon's hijack their assignment.

"Nocturnal squad! Lights out!" Liam adds as they walk away. Noticing everyone looking at him, the rookie explains,

"Nocturnal. Lights out. Night. We're active at night so we shut the lights out on them. Yeah?"

Cedric wraps his arm around his shoulders to move him along. "I like where you were going rook, but let's not say that again ok?"

He looks back at Jason and notices that he is wearing earbuds. "Is he listening to music?"

The wolf glances back to get a look. "Yeah, rumor has it that he needs listen to music to get in his zone. It helps calm him and keeps his mind sharp."

"What kind of music? Probably something dark," Liam asks.

Overhearing their convo, Eriks replies, "If I tell you, I will have to kill you."

"Really?" the rookie asks, shocked.

"Yeah, he would definitely have to kill you," Thea Vost answers.

Cedric moves Liam to keep up the pace and get to the cemetery before it's too late. The street is too busy to keep together, and they eventually get separated. Eriks and his team try to keep up because they want to be the ones who bring Etta in themselves to prove that they are the more superior team.

Cedric and Mason catch up with Lyra who is leading the way at a rapid pace. The vampire slows down a little to be in earshot range to talk with the others. "Guys, we need to think of something. Jason wasn't close with Etta, so the way he's going to handle things won't be pretty for anyone."

"What's the plan then boss?" Mason asks as he is up for anything she suggests.

"I don't know," she answers. Still nervous with her decisions in the past, she hopes one of them would come up with something. "What do you guys think?"

"You don't know or you're doubting yourself?" Mason asks. She looks at him, forgetting that she opened up to him earlier about her struggles. "Any scheme you come up with is a good one. No matter the outcome," the wizard assures.

Cedric notices the look they are giving each other. "Did I miss something?" Knowing from being friends with her for years, the wolf quickly picks up on what was happening. "Lyra, you got this." She looks into his eyes and agrees, confidence slowly coming back.

The vampire thinks hard about the situation. "So, we have to stop Etta from using the stone, but that seems like a no go. We can still try to convince her to let us help her." Hearing Eriks catching up a few yards away, she tries to make something up. "But first we have to deal with the phantom behind us. Ben, I need you to tell Liam to do something."

Pushing his team to keep up, Jason is starting to get irritated when he feels that Lyra is trying to lose him. "What are they up to?" He pushes himself through the crowd. "Where did they go?" They stop to locate them. He looks for the others to help. "Jessy, what do you see?"

The jester climbs effortlessly along the side of a building with her acrobatics to get a good view. "I see that cute white mask guy over there!" she announces, pointing them in the right direction.

Thea Vost rolls her eyes. "How do you know he's cute? Could be a burnt victim under that mask." The goth bandit feels Jason looking at her and she realizes that's why Eriks wears his half mask "Sorry."

"That would be even hotter!" Jessy replies with that twisted fantasy.

Jason gets irritated with his team. "Let's go before they can give us the slip!" They move in on him quickly, following him through an alleyway towards the other side of the building. He sees him standing there watching them approach. Jason feels that something was off. "He's a diversion!" Liam waves and slips them the middle finger as he cloaks himself and runs off. "Retrace our steps! They couldn't have gotten far!" he orders, frustrated from being tricked. "Titan, keep your eyes open!" Jason looks up at the cyclops. "Sorry, I mean eye."

"Nice one fearless leader," Thea says, pushing her way past them to look for Lyra's team.

"Has anyone ever told you that you have an attitude of a teenager?" he replies to her constant remarks.

A short distance away, Lyra and the guys make it to the

cemetery. They approach with caution knowing Etta could have done anything to prevent them from reaching her, like setting any traps.

"Stick together guys," the vampire utters. Lyra makes sure that she is the one to enter first. She hears noises nearby. "Keep your eyes peeled. Things might get a little dangerous."

They hear chanting close by. Walking towards the voices, they see Etta along with Madam Olivia and a dozen others around them. Etta is in the middle of it all. The heart of mare is seen in an opened crypt a few feet from the witches. The night sky gets darker as a hard breeze sweeps through. She starts to open a portal to Hexington Falls.

Mason moves in. "Etta!" The wizard gets her attention. "Please, just talk to me." He holds his hands up, showing her that he isn't there to fight. Hope is still in his heart that if she would just listen to him, then things could work out. "I'm on your side. You just have to give me a chance."

"You left me to rot between four stone walls, why should I listen to you!?" the witch responds. Angered at the thought of being abandoned, she points her wand at her brother-in-law and threatens him, "Leave now or feel the hate that I have!"

Lyra runs out in front of the wizard to protect him. "Etta please, it's us! We're only here to help!"

The witch lowers her wand, humored at what Lyra is doing. "You would risk your life to save him? Do you think he would do the same for you? A low life that only thinks about himself and nobody else?"

"Seems a little rude if you ask me," Ben mumbles to himself.

Mason steps forward and pulls Lyra behind him. Etta smirks. "I guess overtime playing cops and robbers with each other made a connection between you two."

"Etta, I made a whole lot of mistakes in the past and I regret it all. The things I put you and my brother through because I was too selfish to grow up. I'm ashamed of myself," he explains.

No words are spoken right away. Etta is processing in her brain while Mason and Lyra are praying that she will let them in. The witch feels Olivia looking at her from the side. When she turns to her, she notices Cedric creeping his way towards the crypt where the stone is sitting. Etta shoots a bolt at the wolf's feet. "Trying to distract me huh? Well, jokes on you because I had the stone do what I needed from it." She walks into the crypt and grabs the glowing stone, holding it in her hand. "The best part is the academy doesn't explain everything the heart of mare does." The witch points it at Liam, who has made his way back to the group. "It also makes people face their fears!"

A bright red-light shoot towards the rookie and Lyra tries to push him out of the way as fast as she could. As the vampire reaches him, they end up being in the way and both are blasted by the stone.

"Lyra!" Mason cries as he runs toward her. She falls to

the ground unconscious. The wizard slides to the floor beside her and lifts her head to see if she was ok. "Lyra! Lyra, are you ok!? Please answer me!" She doesn't respond. "Cedric, check Liam!" The wolf tries to shake the rookie awake with no success.

Etta makes her way to Mason. "You guys did this to yourselves. Now stay out of my way or the next time will be worse." She grabs a few strands of hair that were hanging off his shoulder without him noticing, and walks away, stopping next to a tomb nearby. The witch places the stone on top of the concrete. "They will be facing what they fear most. You could deactivate the stone, but you will need to wake them up or they will be trapped there forever. Let's see how strong your power is since you bombed the academy." Etta continues walking, but then she remembers one more piece of information. "Oh yeah, one of you will have to go in to help pull them out from their dreams. Not a lot of options on who will go in and who will be out here to turn off the stone."

All the witches make their way towards the exit while Mason runs to the stone. It sits in the palm of his hand. Shocked at what Etta did, he looks up at the wolf. "We got to help them."

Cedric is ready right when Etta insists that he will have to be the one to go in. Mason holds out his hand to let the wolf touch it. The wizard tries a few times to link him with the stone, but he struggles. "Mase, relax. Focus. You got this man," he encourages.

Mason closes his eyes and concentrates on not the stone, but his friends. "Got it! Are you ready?" Cedric takes a deep breath and closes his eyes. The wizard makes his connection with the stone. "Aperta! Aperta! Aperta!"

Cedric holds his eyes closed until the spell is done. "Mase did it work?" He holds them shut for a few seconds longer until he realizes that he isn't holding onto anything anymore. Opening his eyes, he sees that he was somewhere else. The area around him looks to be a city with tall buildings, but at the same time everything seems off. The further he looks; the blurrier things get. "Where am I?" Wandering around the area, he soon realizes that he isn't in Louisiana anymore. "New York? Why am I here?"

He hears a voice from across the street. "Liam, is that you?" The wolf sees the rookie walking around a building as his normal self.

A police officer is acknowledging him. "Liam, I need help inside the building. Come give me a hand."

Liam follows the officer inside, but then stops. "Didn't you tell me to never go inside?" He backs away slowly. "It's you. You're dirty! You tried to kill me!" The rookie begins panicking. "You did this to me!" His voice is filled with anger. He reaches for his gun and shoots at his old partner. As the gun fires, the officer vanishes.

"If you just minded your own business, I wouldn't have to do that to you," his partner says as he appears behind him. "You just couldn't help yourself," he taunts. "You were too busy watching cop tv shows that blinded you to the fact that we aren't all perfect! Sometimes, we must do what we must do to get ahead in life! We don't get paid enough to deal with the crap we have to deal with every day!"

Liam shoots again. He shoots everywhere his partner appears. "I will kill you! Even if that's the last thing I do!" The rookies is angry. His life had been changed forever. He falls to his knees. "My parents. My friends. All taken from me when you turned me into this!"

Cedric watches from a distance, feeling his pain of not being able to live a normal life. He thinks about his past. About his great grandfather leaving Nigeria because of a werewolf bite that had him change every full moon. He fled to London to find someone who said that they could help him break free of his curse. The lady fixed his grandfather, but not for long. After years living without the curse, when Cedric became eighteen, the curse came back after skipping a generation.

"Liam! It's me! This isn't real!" the wolf calls, trying to get his attention.

Liam glances at him, but through his eyes, he only sees his crooked partner. "You will pay for this!" He lifts his gun once again and fires.

"Whoa! Liam calm down, it's me! Cedric!" he tries to convince him. Dodging each shot, trying not to get killed. "Liam!" Finally fed up with being shot at, he rushes his friend and knocks him over. The rookie falls to the floor and drops his weapon. Cedric crawls back up and snaps him out of it. "Hey buddy, it's me. It's Cedric!"

Liam's eyes adjust as he starts to see his friend. "Mama-Bear? Is that really you?" The wolf sighs and nods as he helps him up. Looking around, confused at what is going on, he asks, "What is all this?"

"Your mind is in the stone. It's feeding off what you fear the most by having you come face to face with it," he explains. "We have to find a way out of here."

They try to find a way out but have no luck. An idea pops in Liam's head. "You said it wanted me to come face to face with what I fear?"

"Yeah, but it seems like you got that handled."

"I wasn't afraid of Mark. I have anger towards him, but not fear." He looks up at the abandoned building with a tarp covering the entrance. "I'm afraid of going in there though." He points at the building and Cedric looks. "If movies and tv shows taught me anything, it's that our only way out should be right through there."

Cedric exhales. "Alright, then let's go." He takes a step and notices that Liam is not moving. He nudges his shoulder. "Hey, you got this, ok? You're not alone now." Liam smiles and takes a deep breath as he was feeling safe with his new friend. "Good. Now let's do this together." They walk through the entrance, pushing the tarp aside. A bright white light shines as they pass through.

Coming out the other side, the guys find themselves surrounded by trees. They are in a dark and cold area. Fog takes over the ground as the trees creak from the wind.

"I know this place," Cedric whispers under his breath.

"How can you tell? It's dark and I don't see any signs anywhere."

Cedric walks through the trees, following a dirt path. They make it over a small wooden bridge. "I was here a year ago." He pauses and walks up to a wooden sign. "We're in Sleepy Hollow. This is where Lyra was afraid of going back to."

A thunderous neigh is heard up on the hill along with screaming. Running towards the sound, they see Lyra fighting the headless horseman. Coming from the side, Mitchell arrives, casting a spell on the rider, bounding him with magic.

"Cedric, why are you all the way over there?" Mitch calls.

"Is that Mason's brother? Creepy," Liam whispers.

The guys run over to them as they see the horseman get up and walk towards Mitchell. Cedric tries to yell for them to turn around, but it is too late. The horseman stabs the wizard through the heart and Lyra drops to the ground.

"No! Mitch!" the vampire cries. "No, no, no not again!"

Cedric kneels by Lyra. "Hey, this isn't real, ok?"

She brushes him off. "I can't stop him from dying." The vampire turns and walks the other direction. "This is the tenth time, and he dies no matter what I do." Coming across a wooden bench, she sits with her head down. "There's nothing I can do. With Mitch or you. Something is always going to go wrong, and I won't be able to stop it."

Liam sits next to her. "Look, I get it. A million things can go wrong, but if we try, then that's what makes life worth it. We can't fear what could happen." He tries to add humor to make her feel better. "Hell, I could die from getting a heart attack from eating too many bacon burgers, but I'm going to still eat them anyways." She laughs at his comments. "But what I'm trying to say is, yeah you might lose people on the way, but you shouldn't stop trying to do your job."

Surprised at what Liam had to say, Cedric sits down next to them. "Wow, yeah I agree with rook, things could happen to us anytime and any day. We just can't live in that fear. Plus, if we do things together, we won't have anything to worry about. Life will always try to push you down and remind you of your past, but you just got to forgive yourself and move on. Learn to forgive yourself every time."

Knowing that they were right, she gets up with determination. "You guys are the best. I have been letting the past take control of all my decisions and I have been second guessing myself ever since. Yes, I will always wish for a different outcome with Mitch and if I could go back and save him, I definitely would, but that's not an option." She helps both Cedric and Liam up from the bench. "I know he wouldn't want us to live our lives in regret. He would want us to move on and be there for his wife. Etta's our friend and she needs us. We need to help her no matter what."

236

"I agree and we will, but... We need to find a way out of here so Mason can turn the stone off," Cedric explains.

"Uh... Would that do?" Liam says referring to the tombstone that has Mitchell's name carved on it.

Lyra walks up. "Well, that's messed up for the stone to do, but let's go!" She hops inside the grave first and disappears.

Cedric looks up at Liam, but he notices something in the distance. He hears a howl within the fog and five beastly shadows appear. They walk out and just stand there, watching him with their glowing yellow eyes.

Liam looks back, following Cedric's eyes. He sees what he was looking at and tries to get his attention. "Hey buddy! Cedric! Let's go!"

The wolf snaps out of it and is ready to get out of there. They jump into the grave and make it out of the stone.

"Cedric! Cedric wake up!" he opens his eyes as he heard Ben calling him. "Good, he's awake. Thought I would have to do mouth to mouth for a minute there. Haven't had the chance to brush my teeth or anything yet."

"Somnum!" the wizard yells, deactivating the stone. He watches Lyra as she dusts herself off.

Liam sits up and looks over at Cedric, wondering what they saw. "Hey, what was all that about?"

"It was nothing," he says, trying not to talk about it.

Lyra cracks her neck from the uncomfortable floor her body was lying on. She picks a leaf out from her hair and picks up her staff.

Mason rushes towards her and holds the vampire in his arms. The wizard was worried that she would have been stuck within the stone. Seeing her unconscious body on the floor was devastating. Meanwhile, she felt his muscular arms holding her. Her head rested on his chest. The scent of his cologne was intoxicating to her. She wishes that this moment could last forever. Unfortunately for her, they were still on a mission, so Lyra had to cut his embracement short.

"Awe, that was cute," Ben commented.

"I didn't get any hugs when I woke up from that twisted nightmare," Liam adds. Ben tries to wrap his arm around the invisible man but got swatted away for making things weird.

"Lyra, you good?" Cedric asks, as he was ready to move.

The vampire nods. "Ready to go witch hunting guys?" She winks at Cedric. "Nocturnal Squad... Lights out!"

Thrown off by hearing somebody using his catch phrase, Liam is hyped and ready to go. "Yeah! Let's get that basic witch!"

Cedric slaps his palm against his face as he stands next to their leader. "You just have to encourage him, huh?" The wolf sighs, "Fine, Lights out."

Chapter 19

Etta and her witches leave the cemetery where Lyra and Mason are. Olivia is amazed at what Etta can do and what her and the new witches are capable of. The power that they feel within themselves felt amazing. Unfortunately for them, they are met with another team just outside the walls.

"Hey Thea, don't you just hate running into familiar faces out in public?" Jason announces in an arrogant tone. After tracking down where the nocturnal squad ran off to, they decided to play the waiting game and have Etta come to them.

Olivia steps forward and begins mumbling words in Creole. Other witches follow her lead. Eriks and his team fall to their knees. They start feeling lightheaded and everything around them begins spinning. Their hands collapse to the floor, holding on as if they are about to fall off the earth.

Etta is pleased that the others are picking up the slack, feeling more confident that they all are down for her cause. She kneels by the phantom to whisper in his ear, "You are just a pathetic human. Disrespect me again by standing in my way and I will not hesitate in making this feeling permanent."

He looks up at her, seeing multiple blurry figures of her looking down at him. He tries to build up his strength to talk. Realizing he wants to say something, the witch tilts her head to listen. "I'm... I'm going to kill you."

The witch stands up and walks away as if his words meant nothing. As a being as strong as a witch, she doesn't believe in threats from humans. Leading her new sisters, Etta ignites her wand and reopens the portal with the port-rift once again. Olivia and the others are blown away with more new discoveries. First, the magic, and now a whole supernatural dimension. They march inside and make their way into Hexington Falls where she knows Gabriel will be.

Everyone in Hexington Falls has their annual Halloween celebration interrupted by uninvited guests. Realizing that it is Etta, the mayor instructed his security to sound the alarm. Panic takes to the streets. Everything is becoming pure chaos.

"Gabriel! Show yourself!" she shouts. Olivia stands behind her with the others and they begin chanting. Channeling their shared power from Baron Samedi, they radiate it towards their leader. "Gabriel!"

"Etta Bettings!" Thaddeus calls out. He stands a few yards away from her as Abigail helps clear the streets. Something inside of him made him stay back in town with the knowledge of who she was after. "Mrs. Bettings, I must have you stop this madness before things get out of hand."

She glares at him from the side of her eye. "I advise you to leave captain. You are not the one I want." She turns her back to him in search of the grand wizard.

Captain insists again. "This badge says that I can't leave, so please let's talk this through before somebody gets hurt." He walks slowly towards her. "Please, you don't have to do this. Let me help you."

She scoffs at his remark. "That's all people keep telling me today. You all had your chance to help me and where were all of you? Oh, but once I start being angry and try to do things my own way, everybody wants to help. You all had your chance!" She points back at Olivia and the witches of New Orleans. "My sisters are all the help I need, thank you very much!"

Etta sees Thaddeus getting closer and blasts him with her wand. The captain flies back into a parked bus. The windows smash and the driver jumps out and runs off.

Abigail tries to talk to her, but Etta just signals for her to not say a word. The shapeshifter runs to see if the captain is ok. Blood drips from his skull. "Thaddeus!?"

He lifts his head up and in his weakened voice says, "We need a plan. Try to find where my daughter is and keep everyone off the streets."

*****

Back in New Orleans, Lyra and her team exits the cemetery to follow Etta. On their way out, they run into Jason's team trying to pick themselves up from the floor. "You guys don't look so good. Let me guess, she gave you guys the slip too?"

Eriks gets up to his feet, irritated with the vampires gloating. "We underestimated her, but trust me when I say, that won't happen again."

Giggling in the back is Jessy. "Wow, what a rush! I'm going to have to see if that little witch can do that again!"

"Where did they go?" Mason asks. Seeing their vomit on the floor has the wizard feeling a bit nauseous. "Oh god, we gotta go. Now!"

Wiping her mouth off, Thea answers, "It's too late. They've already opened a portal to Hexington Falls. They're over there doing god knows what."

Without a second thought, Lyra nudges Mason to open a portal. "Let's go. Throw up later."

He gags but keeps himself together to do so. The portal opens and both teams enter. The emergency alarms are ringing, and destruction is seen everywhere. Windows and doors of buildings are smashed in and the city bus close to them was on fire. The street on Halloween night is supposed to be packed with people, but instead it was empty. The city became a ghost town.

"What happened?" Cedric utters. He and Liam sprint to the buildings to see if anyone needs help.

Jason and his team load up their weapons. "Looks as if we're the city's last hope. Better get a move on if we're going to end this thing."

Lyra looks at Eriks with concern. "What do you mean to end this thing?" The vampire watches them switch to lethal rounds in their weapons. "You're not going to try to kill her, are you?"

"Yeah, we're not killing anyone," Mason adds. Even though Etta became a high-level threat, she is still his sister-in-law. The tattoo on his arm begins glowing. "And if you thought we would just sit back and let you, you have another thing coming."

Jason is done arguing on the matter. The phantom has his blaster charged up. "Well then, how about if you guys stop her before we do, then she won't meet her demise so soon."

Mason ignites his wand, preparing to stop Jason before he causes anymore damage. Eriks and his team are ready to go through them to bring an end to the witches terrorizing the city. Lyra tries to calm the wizard down before they all take things too far.

"Uh guys, we... we may have a problem," Liam points behind them, giving everyone a heads up.

Etta stands on top of the burning bus, looking down at them. "If you guys are here to stop me, you're too late." Olivia leads the other witches around the bus and circles around Lyra and her friends. "I gave you guys many chances to leave me alone, but I'm done. Apparently, you want to learn your lesson the hard way."

Lyra and Mason try pleading with her, but she isn't

listening. Her mind is already set on killing Gabriel and making everyone who stands in her way suffer.

"You made sure you got my attention so here I am Mrs. Bettings," a voice calls out from a building next to them. Gabriel walks to the middle of the street, not breaking eye contact with the witch. The grand wizard uncovers the hood from his head and lets his cloak drop to the floor. Rolling up his sleeves, he shows his tattoo glowing. "Well, you've come this far," he taunts waiting for her to make the first move.

"Etta don't do this!" Lyra yells. She walks in the middle of both of their paths. "It wasn't fair to let you grieve by yourself. We all needed each other during that time and still do now. Gabriel just thought if you went in a program without all of us holding you back from progress then–"

Etta stops her talking after hearing those words. "Wait, he told you what? You thought he placed me in a program to get better!?" Her eyes see red. The reason her friends never came was because the grand wizard forbade it. He lied to everyone and left her to deal with her misery alone.

Gabriel hears their conversation and sees Mason looking at him when Etta informs them that she was not in a program to get better. He hopes the rest believe that she was unstable and just saying things to have people feel bad for her.

As he was trying to make sense of it all, Mason sees Etta with all her anger, cast a spell to kill Gabriel. He runs to get Lyra out of the way and barely makes it on time.

Gabriel deflects it with a shield he cast to protect himself. He fights the witch when he summons his wand. The grand wizard returns with another spell, but she blocks it. Everyone moves out of the way because bolts are ricocheting all over the area. Red and yellow streaks light up the sky as they battle.

In the distance, as one spell got deflected and hit a building in the background, Thea spots civilians trapped under ruble. "Titan, help me get those people out of there!" They hurry over to set them free and get them somewhere safe.

As the battle gets more intense, Olivia quickly has the witches get together to hold hands. They chant, transferring their power they were all harnessing that belonged to Baron Samedi. Etta begins getting stronger through them, and Gabriel feels it.

He tries to take shots at them, but they are being protected by Olivia who is casting a shield. Gabriel can't afford casting a stronger spell because he is trying to hold off Etta.

Jason watches everybody standing there, doing nothing to help Gabriel. "It looks as if I have to do this myself." He runs in to make his move on Etta. He adjusts his earbuds and gets himself in position from behind. He aims his barrel at her and pulls the trigger.

Lyra slaps the weapon out of his hand and makes him miss the shot. "I told you before, you're not killing anyone!"

He grunts but is more than happy to deal with her first. Jason throws his weapon at the vampire and charges at her while she deflects it. Catching her off balance, she falls, but launches him over her head. He picks himself up and smirks. Not realizing he placed a stunner on her, Lyra falls to her knees as he pushes the button to shock her. Picking up his blaster, Jason quickly makes his way up to the nearest building. He aims his blaster back at Etta.

Lyra suffers through the pain as she picks herself up. She chases the phantom and pulls out her staff, sweeping his legs, making him miss another shot.

"You're starting to be a pain!" he shouts. The phantom pulls out his knife from his boot and decides to go hand to hand against the vampire.

Mason helps Gabriel hold up the shield by using his wand to add strength to the spell. He uses all his concentration to keep it holding until Cedric is in position. The wolf got ready, "Ced's, now!"

Cedric turns the power level to his wrist tech to fifty percent and launches himself at Etta. Catching her off guard, she has no choice but respond by forfeiting her blast to protect herself from the werewolf. Olivia acts quickly and channels the power to create a barrier to stop him. When he got stopped, all of the other New Orleans witches chanted a spell that picked Cedric into the air and threw him.

Mason sees his friend being tossed so he casts a spell to catch him, "Supernatet!" The wizard gently places the wolf on the ground safely and hears noises from above. He watches as Lyra and Jason fight one another.

Lyra moves too fast for Eriks and he knows that he will lose if he doesn't think of something fast. Playing defense, he dodges her attacks by rolling and using his surroundings to his advantage. Jason notices a propane tank on the rooftop and lures her in. Thinking on his feet, he throws his body over a few crates and places a small detonator on the tank. As the vampire chases him, he gives her the slip and clicks the remote. Before she had a chance to respond, it was too late.

The top of the building explodes, and Lyra flies off. Mason tried to cast another spell to catch her, but he was too slow. Lyra smashes into the lower windows of the building across the street. "Lyra!" he yells, as he ceases his wand to run over to her.

Cedric thinks if he could stop Madam Olivia and the other witches, then Etta will weaken, and Gabriel will be able to put an end to the madness. The wolf runs to attack again, but the voodoo witch isn't going down without a fight.

Madam Olivia reaches out her hands and mumbles in Creole. She makes the wolf collapse to the ground, holding his head in pain. Ben and Liam spring in to help Cedric with the witches. The rookie pulls out his double blasters and fires electric stun rounds. He manages to take down three of the witches, which helps weaken Etta's power against the grand wizard.

Mason runs through the shattered window where Lyra fell through. "Lyra! Where are you?" He sees movement coming from the broken counter next to him. The wizard pushes away

247

the wood and metal off her.

The vampire lifts herself up, coughing from the dust in the air. "Damn, that really hurt." He helps her out of the shop, and she watches the madness that surrounds them. "We need to regroup and come up with a plan to stop this. Are you with me?"

"Yeah, I'm with you."

"Until death?" she asks sarcastically as she starts to move out.

"Maybe even after."

Lyra was thrown off by his remark, but happy he said it. She nudges him and smirks. The wizard looks down at her lips. He looks back up and stares into her eyes. Mason wants to be with her, and he felt that she wanted the same. They forget that they were in the middle of a dangerous event until Jessy came smashing through, riding on top of a wrecking ball. They see Jason and Thea trying to stop her because the jester is doing more damage than helping.

"Maybe we could put a stake through this until later?" she insists. Mason agrees and they continue with their plan.

"You are a fool if you think this will end well for you," Gabriel shouts. The wizard knows that he can get into her head. One little mistake and he will be able to take her down. He pushes her more. "You are just a little girl that doesn't know how to control her feelings. All that power and you still challenge me with only child games."

Etta pulls back her blast, knowing that he is more experienced with face-to-face combat. She thinks to herself that if she takes advantage of his old age, then she might be able to catch him with his guard down. She launches herself from side to side, casting spells from all angles. Noticing that Gabriel is struggling to adjust to her strikes, she sees an opening and shoots a blast to his ribs.

Olivia sees Gabriel go down as the glow from his tattoo fades. He struggles with casting a strong enough shield to protect himself. She and the others wait in anticipation for Etta to finish what she started.

Lyra and Mason meet with Cedric and the others in a corner of a shop. "Ok guys, we need a plan and think of one quickly."

"Well, we need to knock out a few more witches because they're the ones giving her all that power," Cedric explains.

"We'll have to keep both sides distracted if we want to succeed. Have them not work as a team like we've done before that got our butts kicked," Mason adds.

Liam offers himself up for the cause. "Fine, you guys become their targets and I'll do my *thang*." He sees the confusion on everyone's face, so he goes into detail. "Sneak around putting everyone in a sleeper hold one by one."

An idea sparks inside of Lyra. While the others did not take the rookie seriously, she thinks of something that could work. The vampire gathers everyone in closer as she explains her idea.

Etta walks up to Gabriel with a smug look on her face. Victory is in reach as he tries limping away from her. Blood begins seeping through his clothing. The witch toys with him by zapping him from her wand. She kicks him over to have his back against the floor so she can look at his face one last time. Her wand lifts in the air as she is ready for one last blow. "This is for Mitch."

Mason casts a shield over Gabriel, preventing her from killing him. "Sorry Etta, but I can't let you do that to yourself."

In rage at his actions, she points her wand towards him. "You're not going to let me have the satisfaction of getting my revenge!?"

She fires at him, but he deflects everything. Mason is ready to fight, but as he begins to cast a spell at her, a sharp pain courses through his chest. Yelling in pain, he collapses on the floor as another sharp pain is felt, but this time it is in his leg. One of the witches comes around holding a voodoo doll with the wizard's hair attached. Pins are seen poking out of the doll's chest and leg. Etta grabs the doll from the witch's hand and pulls a pin out from her hair to slowly stab it through its hand. "Did you think you had a chance? Did a little practice with magic and had the audacity to think you could go against me!?"

Mason stands on his knees. "I just needed to distract you."

Etta turns to the grand wizard, but his body is missing. In

the distance, Cedric is dragging him to safety. The witch takes a step to go after him, but she is met by her brother-in-law who refuses to let her go after them.

"Out of my way, Mason!" she screams. Etta is over letting him ruin her plans.

"Sorry, but this all ends here," he points his wand at her, telling her to surrender.

She scoffs. "Why are you protecting him? I know deep down that he had something to do with my husband's murder! Your brother!"

He stands silent and turns his head back to where Cedric is aiding Gabriel. "Well, if that's true, we will deal with him. The right way."

Etta tries to recruit him to her side. "Join me. Join me and I will prove to you that Gabriel killed Mitchell or at least had something to do with his murder. We will get justice for him, and we can finally mourn peacefully knowing that we did right by your brother."

He considers her offer. If what she's saying is true, then it will explain why his brother's spirit never appeared during the day of the dead. If his soul is being held against his will, then he would have to do something about it.

Watching him struggle processing her words, she takes the opening to strike. Mason struggles but jumps out of the way and strikes back at her. They both share blasts at one another. He strikes her hand, and she drops the doll on the floor. As she tries to pick it up, the wizard shoots a fiery rope that fires out of a lighter from his belt, landing on the doll. The magic grabs it like a magnet and he reels it back to him. She sees how far he has come from how he used to be with his magic. Since the last time she saw him until now, he made major improvements. Mixing his new magic abilities along with his magical objects that he uses, the witch knows that she may have underestimated her brother-in-law.

Olivia sees Etta struggling and orders the other witches to focus and give Etta everything they have. Before they have a chance to do anything, they are all thrown back by a firehose that Ben connects to a hydrant. "Sorry ladies, that was a lot stronger than I imagined," he apologizes. He turns off the water and drops the hose.

Madam Olivia gets back up and mumbles words in Creole. Ben falls to the floor in pain as his head pounds. She walks up to him and rips a piece of hair from his head. The witches quickly make their escape while everything falls apart.

Sparks are flying as Mason and Etta duel in the streets. Each time their bolts strike, loud bangs are heard. Gabriel and Cedric feel every vibration of it under their feet. Ben gets up and hides by the wolf until Lyra and Liam get back.

Etta is done playing this game with the wizard. She begins retreating as he thinks he was winning. The witch sends one last blast to push him back and it worked. Mason blocks the blast and when he goes to do another strike, she vanishes.

As silence fills the air, Cedric looks around the corner to

see Mason by himself. "Guys, wait here," he instructs. Coming out in the open, the wolf turns on his tech to see if he can sense any of the witches.

Ben rubs his head. "I hope being in a dead body that I could still grow hair to cover this patch that psycho left me with."

Gabriel is too disgusted to pay any mind to the undead human. The wizard did not expect all the newer witches to come together so quickly. Having the whole scenario play over in his head, his eyes catch a figure behind the new guy.

Ben follows Gabriel's eyes and sees Olivia walking towards them. "Hey, stealing my hair? How low could you really go?"

"Six feet under," she utters. Olivia pulls a doll from her back and displays it in her hand. The doll has button eyes and human hair glued on top of it.

Ben squints his eyes to look at it, but the witch grabs its leg and jabs a small pin in it. He grabs his thigh tightly as a sharp pain shoot through his body. He yells in agony as she pierces another pin in the doll's arm. Mason and Cedric run over to see what was going on, but when they get closer, Olivia grabs the doll's head and twists it, snapping Ben's neck.

"No!" they yell. Cedric has a flashback of how Mitchell got killed and the same feeling comes flooding back.

Olivia uses what she has left of Baron's power and pushes the guys with a jolt. She reaches out her hand and rolls her eyes to the back of her head as she chants a spell. Spirits appear around them as they begin chanting. The guys look at each other knowing that they are screwed. After a couple of words, she feels a metal clamp on her arm.

As she adjusts her eyes, Lyra is standing in front of her with a smirk on her face. "Yeah, you won't be doing any of that anymore." The witch tries to cast a spell but can't. "This is a power dampener. It's like a handcuff, but for magical people."

"I highly doubt you have another one of those," Etta interrupts. Her hand is glowing from her wand. She walks out from the shadows with her eyes glued to Gabriel's. Her arm rises as she points at him. "You dug your grave and now you lay in it!"

Lyra steps between them to convince her to stop. "Etta please, reconsider this. Killing him won't bring your husband back!"

Etta never breaks eye contact with the wizard. She hears what the vampire has to say, but she's done talking. She sees Lyra put out her hand to her. She stares at it for a moment, then looks up at her. "Nothing you say will stop me from killing him or anyone who stands in between us."

She pulls her hand back to her chest. "I really hoped you wouldn't say that. Nocturnal Squad, lights out," she exhales.

Etta feels a sharp pinch in her neck. Her hand grabs where the pain is and feels a pen-like object. Looking at what she was holding between her fingers, she sees a syringe. Liam uncloaks himself and walks towards the vampire. Etta's eyes are wide open, trying to process what was happening. Her body is failing her. Her eyes are getting heavier by the second. Collapsing to the floor, Lyra grabs her and lays her down gently.

Captain Vansin storms the area with multiple rangers in search of the other witches. "I want them all alive and placed in containment!" He sees his daughter holding Etta in her arms and Olivia in cuffs. "Is it safe to say all of this is over?"

Lyra nods her head. "Yeah, it's finally over."

"Well, let's get a crew here to get all this cleaned up so we can figure out what the next move is," Thaddeus says.

Rangers end up locating all the runaway witches and place power dampeners on them. "Load them all up in the truck!" Hunter orders. He watches Lyra as she speaks with her father. The vampire gets tapped on the shoulder. He turns to see one of the mayors' assistants holding a letter.

Mason sits Etta in a transporter to be escorted somewhere she will be safe from herself and others. He imagines his brother would be crushed seeing what his wife has become. "Hey, I'm going to help you get through this," he whispers to her unconscious body. The door closes and the vehicle drives off.

A paramedic helps Ben get back up with his head completely turned around. "Ah geez, I'm going to be feeling this in the morning for sure." The medic escorts him to the pop-up tent where they are taking care of the wounded.

Liam sits on the bed beside him, shaking a bottle of pills.

"Ouch, that looks painful. Want an aspirin?" He watches as Abigail walks over. "A librarian and a nurse? Don't tell me, you're building a campaign to become the next mayor too?"

Abigail smacks him in the head with her chart, making it look like an accident. "Whoops, I'm sorry, I guess you could cross off being a *good* nurse." She examines Ben's neck. "Well, I have an idea."

Right before he has the chance to ask, the shapeshifter transforms her arms like an ogre and snaps his neck back around. "Ahhh! That hurts!" The pain only hurts for a moment until he feels his head back to where it should be. "Oh, that actually feels a lot better! I guess I'm lucky to be a zombie, huh?"

"Now get some rest. I need to find Thaddeus, but I'll check up on you later" she orders.

A large group of sentinels swarm the area. Thaddeus rushes towards them to block them from interfering with the crime scene. He is cut off by Hunter. "Captain, I have urgent news for you." He hands the letter for him to read. "Sir, apparently the mayor granted Gabriel permission to take Etta and all of the witches in their care."

The captain is baffled by the news. "What!? Why? This happened in our city! They should be under our watch since Etta was able to give them the slip before. Under their watch!"

Overhearing the captain's displeasure, Gabriel approaches. "I must say, you all seem to have done an incredible job here, but I'm afraid we must take it from here now captain."

His voice seems honest, but reading between the lines, they sense that there's something more here than he leads on.

Thaddeus gives the grand wizard an angry look. He doesn't know why the mayor granted him permission, but something was off. With everything that has been going on, he knows that the decision here is going to bite them at the end.

Lyra and her team shook their heads. All that hard work to finally have Etta in their custody just to have her ripped away from them. They wanted to help her. Get the witch back to herself but now that chance seem less likely.

Jason scoffs at the mayor's decision and leaves the scene with his team. Even he knew how crappy that order was. Thea was just happy to leave before their team got blamed for destroying half the block because of Jessy's wild idea. Titan places the jester in the truck as she was strapped in a straitjacket.

Abigail rubs Thaddeus on the back as she knows how upset the captain is.

******

Gabriel enters a black SUV as soon as it pulls up. A young wizard closes the door as he enters. A figure seated in the back row pulls down his hood. "Did everything go as planned?"

"Yes, it did Ian. It was a success indeed," the grand wizard replies without looking back at him. Ian smiles with his dirty yellow teeth as his master is pleased and hands over the heart of mare that is wrapped inside a dirty cloth that he snatched from the captain's men. Another figure appears beside Gabriel.

"And as for you, it was quite careless of you to be caught on camera, Cain."

The glowing blue apparition takes form. "Careful Gabriel, we don't want you to forget who you are speaking to."

"All I'm saying is that we need to be careful now. I've got word that they suspect the Higher Power now. We don't need to draw any more attention. Especially from the captain," the wizard explains.

Cain studies his face. "Don't you worry about Thaddeus. The cult will get ready for the next phase. It's almost time for the Higher Power to come into the light to bring in even more followers." He looks forward at the road as they drive away. "The First Borns Shall Rise Again," Gabriel and Ian chant. Cain smirks as his eyes reflect an emerald glow.

Chapter 20

Three days later

Hexington Falls is getting back to normal. Halloween started off right but ended as a nightmare. The day of the dead came and went. Many spent the day at the cemetery, spending time with the spirits of loved ones who had passed. Lyra and her friends are getting ready for their weekend away like they planned back in New Orleans. They meet up at headquarters before leaving.

"Lyra, are you ready?" Mason asks, holding a red backpack in his hands, waiting for the vampire.

"Almost. Where's Ben?"

"He'll meet us in a bit. He's coming back from Sacred Hills. Gabriel did me a solid by helping Ben's spirit become permanently sealed within his body to stop him from becoming a raging psycho." He sees her eyes wander to the gold medal that hangs around his neck. "Oh, this thing? The mayor and I had a little chat. We agreed that if I keep helping out, he'll talk to your dad about a permanent position here."

She tosses her black duffle bag at him. "Let me find the

others so we can head out, Mr. good citizen." The vampire winks at him and continues towards the elevator. As the bell rings for the lower level, the doors open. Liam is having his suit evaluated by the doctor. Cedric is out in the hallway, watching through the window. "Hey, are you ready?"

"Yeah, almost," he replies. The door behind them opens as Samara is holding a moonrock from storage.

"Thanks." He switches out the one that had gotten damaged during their mission and replaces it with the one he had before.

She blushes when he touches her hand. Caught up in the moment, Samara doesn't grab the damaged rock properly and drops it. "Oh shoot, luckily that one is already broken." Embarrassed, she kneels to pick it up.

Cedric quickly kneels at the same time and bumps heads with her. "I'm so sorry! I was trying to help."

They laugh as they look into each other's eyes. Goosebumps form on his skin. His gets choked up as he just stands there.

The vampire snickers at this cringing scene. "So, I'm going to meet you back upstairs. Give the two of you a little time." She walks back towards the elevator.

Samara gets up, embarrassed that she forgot somebody was standing there. "I should get back to work. I have a lot of paperwork to do. I hope you have a fun team-bonding weekend though."

Turning to walk away, Cedric quickly grabs her hand. "Hey, wait a minute." She looks back at him with anticipation. "When I get back, would you maybe be down for dinner?"

She smiles, parting her red lips, showing off her beautiful smile. "As a date?" The wolf nods, scared to say another word in fear of his voice cracking with how nervous he feels. "Yes! I mean, yeah. I would like that a lot," she quickly replies, trying to keep calm but screaming with excitement on the inside.

Cedric leaves to meet up with his partner as he sees both her and Liam watching, trying to act like they weren't being nosey. The rookie can't hold in his excitement. "My man! Taking yourself off the market, officially. I guess I'm the lone wolf in a world full of beautiful ladies."

Lyra gives him a light jab on the shoulder. "I'm proud of you. Now if you hurt her, I will hunt you down."

He laughs. "Thanks Fangs, and don't worry about that. She's the tough one."

The bell rings and the elevator doors open. Frankie walks in, informing them of the orders he was given. "Sorry Lyra, but your father would like to see you and Cedric before you leave."

They glance at each other, not knowing what it is about. Liam gets off in the lobby and the others follow Frankie to the fifth floor where his office is. He stood silent, not answering any questions they asked about his orders. They reach the level and walk through the hall to the door.

As they enter, Lyra sees her father, Hunter and Abigail in

the office. All eyes are on them as they open the door. They're all scattered around the room with a serious look on their faces. Dr. Stein enters behind to join the meeting.

"Please my dear, come in," Thaddeus greets, assisting them to have a seat.

Lyra glances around the room again. "Is everything ok? Is there another recruit?"

Her father takes a seat at his desk and looks into her curious eyes. "What I'm about to tell you, cannot leave this room. Do you understand?" She looks at him, concerned. She nods and he continues, "I'm afraid that we may have bigger problems at hand." He clears his throat. "We have reason to believe that the cult, Higher Power, has returned to Hexington Falls."

"Wait, what's the Higher Power?" Cedric asks.

Abigail volunteers to explain. "The Higher Power was a notorious group many centuries ago who believed that us, the living of the supernatural, shouldn't be hiding from the human world. They believed that we are superior to humans and that we all should be out in the open, ruling."

Cedric looks over to Lyra to read her thoughts. "How do you know that they are here?"

Thaddeus opens his drawer. He pulls out photos and smacks them on the table. "Because of this." They look at the picture, but they still aren't catching on. "Look behind Gabriel and the mayor." They look harder and see a figure standing there.

She looks up at her father to explain. "It's a spirit. Cedric mentions in his report that the stranger, whom Etta met at a nightclub, had an emerald glow in his eyes. Danny, the night Mitchell was killed, helped a Djinn who he reported had the same reflection in her eyes as well. Look at the spirit in this picture again."

The mood gets darker as Lyra looks closer. "Emerald! Wait, what does this mean?"

"Are you trying to say that Etta was right about Gabriel?" Cedric asks.

"If she was right then that means Mitchell's murder was planned," Lyra mumbles with her voice cracking. "But I don't understand, why kill him?"

"We are not sure at this moment. Danny was assigned to be the wizard on your team at Sleepy Hollow, but I'm assuming this spirit had other plans. Avoiding him from going and having Mitchell go instead. Whatever the reason for it though, it's not good," the doctor answers.

"Well, if we know Gabriel's guilty, then what's stopping us from arresting him right now?" Cedric asks.

"We cannot make a move on Gabriel unless we have more proof. Going after him now could possibly cause a war and I'm not trying to lose thousands of lives. His sentinel army took a vow of following the grand wizard till the end unless he is proven guilty. We have to be smart," the captain explains.

Lyra doesn't know what to think. So much information to

process right before she goes off on vacation. "How do we stop this cult then?"

"We have to first figure out who is part of this group and build an alliance with people that we can trust," Abigail informs. "They were a popular group amongst the citizens in every city back then."

"Well, me and my team are in, so let me know whatever you need," she offers.

"Maybe not all of us." Everyone looks at Cedric. "Mason did show up a few days ago hiding a spirit in his bag. Ben."

The room fills with whispers. Thaddeus is caught off guard with the news. He looks at his daughter and then moves towards the window to think. He didn't know that Ben was a ghost. Lyra didn't tell him. He thought that Ben was an undead civilian.

Lyra tries to defend the wizard by explaining that he shows no signs of being in a cult and that Ben is harmless. She does all she can to convince her father to trust what she is saying.

"No!" her father yells. Everyone got silent. Thaddeus turns around and sits in his chair. "As of now, we are to believe that the cult walks among us. Everyone we walk by could be a potential threat to us. We will only trust the faces we see here as of now."

"What about Liam? Samara?" Cedric asks.

"We will keep our eyes on them until we know for sure

that we can trust them," the captain informs. His eyes travel to Lyra. "That includes Mr. Bettings." Everyone agrees with his decision. Thaddeus dismisses them until the next meeting. Lyra and Cedric get up to leave but are stopped by her father. "Lyra, I need you to trust me. I also need to trust you."

Her voice cracks with anger. "Why do I need to gain your trust? After everything we've been through?"

"I'm sorry, but I know you fancy the boy and take it from me, love can make you blind to the other person's intentions," he expresses. She agrees not to mention any of this to anybody. He hugs her and lets her leave his office.

Returning to the lobby, they both catch Mason talking to Liam and Ben. Their eyes connect as they grab their bags. The vampire looks around the building and catches eyes glancing at them. Suddenly, everyone became a suspect. People they've known for years seem mischievous.

Hunter approaches from behind and wraps his arm around her, informing her that he's going to stay close by to figure out which side Mason is on. That he was ordered by her father to join them on their weekend trip and after, he will be assigned to her team.

Mason watches as the two vampires walk towards the exit. Before walking out the doors, Hunter kisses Lyra's forehead. He grabs her hand and tells her that he is going to quickly pack his bag. Mason feels sick to his stomach. The wizard doesn't understand what the hell is going on.

Cedric follows Lyra outside into the crowded streets and everyone's eyes seem to be on them. From the shopkeepers to the civilians just enjoying their day. Some look as if they are whispering to each other, plotting against them. They all look guilty and that is when the city became dimmer. Being swarmed with people they couldn't trust anymore. Any one of them can be their downfall. Being cautious is an understatement. At this point, it felt like swimming with sharks. Whatever the captain is planning to stop Gabriel and his followers, they both hope that it happens sooner rather than later. Or at least figure out who they can trust.

The worst part about it all is that she has to now take a step back from her feelings with Mason because it was true what her father said Love *can make you blind to the other person's intention.*

THE END

Miguel T. Pintos is of Puerto Rican decent. Born in the Bronx, NY, he moved down to south Florida when he was a child. As a kid, Miguel enjoyed reading comic books like X-Men and Spider-Man and watch movies like Ghostbusters and Star Wars.

During Middle School, he was teased for liking Star Wars, so for years he decided to hide his passion for it and like whatever was IN at the time. After he had his first child, his passion from his childhood slowly came back and Miguel was proud to show everyone that he wasn't ashamed to love all the nerdy things that he grew up loving.

Miguel's love for everything from his childhood has helped him create his own story. Hexington Falls is the first official book that he wrote with many more from the series to come.

"Love what you love and don't let anyone tell you otherwise."

Milton Keynes UK
Ingram Content Group UK Ltd.
UKHW020705290424
441924UK00017B/1027